QUORNE RETURNS

Borgo Press Books by JOHN RUSSELL FEARN

*1,000-Year Voyage: A Science Fiction Novel * Anjani the Mighty: A Lost Race Novel* (Anjani #2) * *Black Maria, M.A.: A Classic Crime Novel* (Black Maria #1) * *A Casebook for Brutus Lloyd * The Crimson Rambler: A Crime Novel * Don't Touch Me: A Crime Novel * Dynasty of the Small: Classic Science Fiction Stories * The Empty Coffins: A Mystery of Horror * The Fourth Door: A Mystery Novel * From Afar: A Science Fiction Mystery * Fugitive of Time: A Classic Science Fiction Novel * The G-Bomb: A Science Fiction Novel * The Genial Dinosaur* (Herbert the Dinosaur #2) * *The Gold of Akada: A Jungle Adventure Novel* (Anjani #1) * *Here and Now: A Science Fiction Novel * Into the Unknown: A Science Fiction Tale * Last Conflict: Classic Science Fiction Stories * Legacy from Sirius: A Classic Science Fiction Novel * The Man from Hell: Classic Science Fiction Stories * The Man Who Was Not: A Crime Novel * Manton's World: A Classic Science Fiction Novel * Moon Magic: A Novel of Romance* (as Elizabeth Rutland) * *The Murdered Schoolgirl: A Classic Crime Novel* (Black Maria #2) * *One Remained Seated: A Classic Crime Novel* (Black Maria #3) * *One Way Out: A Crime Novel* (with Philip Harbottle) * *Pattern of Murder: A Classic Crime Novel * Reflected Glory: A Dr. Castle Classic Crime Novel * Robbery Without Violence: Two Science Fiction Crime Stories * Rule of the Brains: Classic Science Fiction Stories * Shattering Glass: A Crime Novel * The Silvered Cage: A Scientific Murder Mystery * Slaves of Ijax: A Science Fiction Novel * Something from Mercury: Classic Science Fiction Stories * The Space Warp: A Science Fiction Novel * A Thing of the Past* (Herbert the Dinosaur #1) * *Thy Arm Alone: A Classic Crime Novel* (Black Maria #4) * *The Time Trap: A Science Fiction Novel * Vision Sinister: A Scientific Detective Thriller * Voice of the Conqueror: A Classic Science Fiction Novel * What Happened to Hammond? A Scientific Mystery * Within That Room!: A Classic Crime Novel*

THE GOLDEN AMAZON SAGA

1. *World Beneath Ice* * 2. *Lord of Atlantis* * 3. *Triangle of Power* * 4. *The Amethyst City* * 5. *Daughter of the Amazon* * 6. *Quorne Returns* * 7. *The Central Intelligence* * 8. *The Cosmic Crusaders* * 9. *Parasite Planet* * 10. *World Out of Step* * 11. *The Shadow People* * 12. *Kingpin Planet* * 13. *World in Reverse* * 14. *Dwellers in Darkness* * 15. *World in Duplicate* * 16. *Lords of Creation* * 17. *Duel with Colossus* * 18. *Standstill Planet* * 19. *Ghost World* * 20. *Earth Divided* * 21. *Chameleon Planet* (with Philip Harbottle)

QUORNE RETURNS

THE GOLDEN AMAZON SAGA, BOOK SIX

JOHN RUSSELL FEARN

Edited by Philip Harbottle

THE BORGO PRESS

MMXIII

QUORNE RETURNS

FIRST BORGO PRESS EDITION

Published by Wildside Press LLC

www.wildsidebooks.com

DEDICATION

For Dave Gibson

CONTENTS

THE GOLDEN AMAZON, by Philip Harbottle. . . .9

CHAPTER ONE: Quorne Takes Over 17

CHAPTER TWO: Plan Is Exposed. 24

CHAPTER THREE: Too Late to Act 33

CHAPTER FOUR: The Big Break. 41

CHAPTER FIVE: Ready for Action 50

CHAPTER SIX: Important Discovery 59

CHAPTER SEVEN: Step by Step 67

CHAPTER EIGHT: Temporary Halt 75

CHAPTER NINE: So Far, So Good 84

CHAPTER TEN: Back to Earth 92

CHAPTER ELEVEN: "Up Against a Problem" . 100

CHAPTER TWELVE: Trivial Errand 107

CHAPTER THIRTEEN: Quickly Dealt With . . 114

CHAPTER FOURTEEN: Preparing for Revenge 123

CHAPTER FIFTEEN: A Miscalculation. 131

CHAPTER SIXTEEN: Visitors from Another
World 139
CHAPTER SEVENTEEN: Puzzled Trio. 147
CHAPTER EIGHTEEN: Unable to Escape . . . 157
CHAPTER NINETEEN: Trouble Ahead 165
CHAPTER TWENTY: Back in 'Form' 174
CHAPTER TWENTY-ONE: An Even Start. . . 184
ABOUT THE AUTHOR 193

THE GOLDEN AMAZON

by Philip Harbottle

In 1943 British writer John Russell Fearn decided to quit writing for the American pulp science fiction magazines, and to concentrate instead on books for the English market. Within a very few years he became established as a leading novelist in several genres, not only science fiction, but also mystery and detective fiction, and westerns.

His first new SF novel, *The Golden Amazon*, was published by World's Work in April 1944. In this story, a little girl of three years of age is made the subject of an idealistic scientist's illegal glandular experiments. The scientist's dream is to end world wars by creating a woman devoid of the usual lusts and frailties of mankind, who upon reaching maturity would institute a benign scientific rule. But the apparently successful experiment has a flaw: it instills into the girl a hatred for all men, and a ruthless cruelty. Her supernatural scientific gifts enable her to master atomic power, and practically leads her to destroy the world. She breaks the will and strength of men, and elevates women to positions of wealth and power. She also discovers human synthesis, and by this means she is able to escape retribution when she is eventually overthrown. She is seen to collapse and die, a victim of consuming ketabolism, echoing the memorable finale of Rider Haggard's *She*. In actuality, it was only her synthetic image, and this paved the way for the *Golden Amazon Returns*, and further sequels

Fearn sold reprint rights in the first novel to the prestigious Canadian magazine, the Toronto *Star Weekly*. The magazine carried a special Comics Supplement, the centre section of which was a 'complete novel', published in newspaper format. Aimed at a general readership, the novels were written by the top popular novelists of the day, including John Dickson Carr, Ellery Queen, and P. G. Wodehouse. They sold hundreds of thousands of copies, and the novels were syndicated to several American newspapers in the Maine and New York areas. The Amazon novels enjoyed extraordinary popularity (especially with Canadian housewives), and ran for the next sixteen years following the appearance of the first novel in the March 3, 1945 issue, ending with Fearn's sudden death in September 1960, aged only fifty-two. His final two Amazon novels appeared posthumously.

During Fearn's lifetime, only the first six novels were published in British hardcover editions from the World's Work in England, after appearing in the *Star Weekly*. This was because the publishers discontinued their entire fiction line in 1954. However, the Amazon novels continued to appear in the *Star Weekly*, eventually notching up twenty-four titles.

Fearn had resold paperback rights to the Canadian publisher Harlequin Books, but after publishing only the first three titles, they stopped publishing SF and other genre fiction to concentrate on their famous Romances line.

Meanwhile, as early as 1949, Fearn had realized that the Amazon series had the potential to run indefinitely. This presented him with a problem, however. The 'origin story' of the Golden Amazon was conceived and actually set during the Second World War. Subsequent novels were written during the war and the immediate postwar period, and projected their stories only a few decades into the future.

He very astutely realized that to keep ahead of reality, he needed to move the Amazon *further* into the future—first into the outer solar system, and thence to the stars. So with the seventh novel, he introduced a new main character, Abna of Atlantis—someone as equally intelligent, and even stronger than herself. These dynamics provided him with an *interstellar* canvas, thus ensuring that the series would remain ahead of reality.

Fearn's strategy was a great success, and the Amazon novels retained their popularity, ending only with his tragically early death in 1960. By then he had written a further twenty Amazon novels, and made preliminary notes for his next (which would later be written by Fearn's biographer, Philip Harbottle).

Long after Fearn's death, his entire Amazon series

would eventually see print from the pioneering US small press Gryphon Books in limited paperback editions, and later by the Canadian Battered Silicon Dispatch Box small press in their hardcover Omnibus series.

This new Borgo Press paperback series will be the first trade edition of all twenty-one of these later novels by Fearn, beginning with the seventh novel in the original series. First published in 1949 as *Conquest of the Amazon*, I have edited it slightly as *World Beneath Ice* (The Golden Amazon Saga, Book One) so that it can be read and enjoyed by new readers who may be totally unfamiliar with what had gone before. Subsequent novels have also been slightly edited for modern readers.

The publishers hope that this new series may create many more "fans of the Amazon." Meanwhile, any reader interested in seeking out the earlier six Golden Amazon novels will find that they are readily available on the internet, and in numerous earlier paperback and hardcover editions.

* * * * * * * * *

To date, readers can enjoy the following new Borgo Press editions:

Book One: *World Beneath Ice*

In destroying the threat of an alien invasion, the Golden Amazon had inadvertently caused a decline in the sun's heat, encasing Earth in an ice sheet that threatens to eliminate humanity. The Amazon encounters Abna, a descendant of Atlantis, stronger and even more scientifically advanced than she, and the ruler of an Atlantean colony still surviving in a protected environment on Jupiter. She refuses his offer of marriage, but agrees to form an alliance in order to restore the sun and save the Earth. One thing that Abna has not told the Amazon is that all the females of his race have been wiped out by a bacilli infection....

Book Two: *Lord of Atlantis*

A gigantic ridge of land rises from the Atlantic floor, causing massive tidal waves on either side of the ocean. Even stranger, both England and America are then assailed by an invasion of prehistoric monsters! A gigantic domed city rests on the newly risen plateau, whilst out in space an alien spacecraft orbits the Earth. Such are the mysteries and challenges facing the Golden Amazon, self-appointed governess of Earth, as she struggles to unravel the maze of mystery that was the deadly legacy of Atlantis!

Book Three: *Triangle of Power*

The marriage of Violet Ray Brant—better known as The Golden Amazon—and Abna of Atlantis should have ushered in an era of peace and scientific prosperity to the people of Earth. But an unexpected turn of events finds Abna betrayed and marooned on a satellite of Jupiter, and the Amazon flung far beyond the Solar System. With Earth's two protectors removed, the planet is now at the mercy of another Atlantean, the master scientist Sefnor Quorne....

Book Four: *The Amethyst City*

The metaphysical union of the Amazon and Abna results in the mental creation of a fully mature daughter—Viona. Quorne, still struggling for domination, forces Viona into a marriage ceremony, and impregnates her. But with the intervention of Tarnec Brodix, a super-mind from an external universe, Quorne and Viona are separately flung into an ultra-dimensional limbo. Abna chooses to follow after his daughter, leaving the Amazon to brood over the disaster, alone in the Amethyst City of Saturn.

Book Five: *Daughter of the Amazon*

A miscalculation by the super-mathematician Tarnec Brodix destroys his universe, and the fault spreads into the Earth universe in the form of a Dark Tide of Absolute Nothingness. Unable to save himself, Brodix transfers his knowledge into the one mind powerful enough to receive it: that if Sefian, the son who has been born to Viona and Quorne. Sefian rapidly evolves, and, no longer human, after saving the Earth universe, vanishes into the greater universe, to seek new challenges. Then the Amazon is confronted with a further puzzle—a large section of the planet Neptune is discovered to be an exact duplicate of the Earth!

CHAPTER ONE
QUORNE TAKES OVER

The slim man with the jet-black hair and heliotrope-colored eyes stood thinking. Then he began to inspect his dusty uniform, marked from the moment he had been thrown in the dust by the superwoman, the Golden Amazon of Earth. He smiled a little as he began to move.

A chance traveler through the Solar System who had lost his planetary bearings would have declared upon landing upon a particular portion of this planet that he was on Earth—but he would have been mistaken. Here was the planet Neptune, last of the outermost giants and a world of surprises.

Here existed the bacteria race of high intelligence, originally born in the poisonous wastes of Uranus, whose amazing powers of adaptability made them capable of assuming any form by electrical processes. Here on this distant world existed a duplicate of conditions reigning on Earth, even to the extent of vast numbers of its inhabitants being 'carbon copied' to resemble the originals.

Here, too, existed a man who was the greatest menace

the Solar System had ever known, a man believed to be dead—Sefner Quorne of Jupiter.

Quorne left the spaceport where he had his final unsuccessful brush with the Golden Amazon, her husband Abna of Jupiter, and their daughter Viona. He walked through streets that were indistinguishable from those of futuristic London, and concluded his journey at the gigantic edifice duplicating the one in normal London from where there was administered government.

Head of the government of this mystery world of Neptune was Dral, looking exactly like an Earthman since he was patterned after one. He also looked to be in an extremely bad temper when Sefner Quorne was shown into his big private office.

"Well, captain, what have you to say for yourself?" Dral demanded bitterly, using his own language. "You, the captain of the guard, allowed those three captives to escape! Why didn't you order an immediate corps of space machines to pursue them?"

"Because it would have been useless," Sefner Quorne replied calmly. "The Golden Amazon used every scrap of energy which her spaceship, the *Ultra*, possessed, and that meant they flew into the void at a speed infinitely greater than any pursuers could stand."

"You seem to have forgotten," Dral snapped, "how dangerous they can be now they've escaped. This secret territory of ours on this far-flung planet will be secret no longer."

"Correct," Quorne admitted. "Had I known those

three people had arrived here, I might have been able to warn you against the impossibility of holding them. Their science and mental powers sets them in a class apart."

"They are only Earth people."

"You are mistaken, Dral. The Golden Amazon alone is Earth-born, and she became a superwoman both physically and mentally because of a scientist's experiment when she was an infant. As for her husband Abna, he was formerly the ruler of Jupiter, and his strength and intelligence outclass even those of his wife. Viona, the younger woman, is the product of both of them, and she was not born in the normal material way. She is the product of unified intellects and pure scientific conception. There," Quorne finished, "you face danger, Dral, as I have good reason to know."

"You! A captain of my defence guard! Don't be ridiculous."

Quorne smiled coldly. "You believe I am that. You believe I am one of your own bacterial race who has taken on the pattern of an Earth being?"

"I know you are, because I was present in the laboratory when you assumed your present identity. We came here because our own world was too limiting. You know that by thought processes we absorbed the vibrations of people on Earth and thereby duplicated ourselves in their images, so that we could have physical bodies better suited to our needs. You know that basically we are bacteria people, the most indestructible and yet the most adaptable form of life—"

"I know, yes," Quorne agreed, "but there is much more to the story than that. When one of your race absorbed my image from Earth without my knowledge, he became Captain of the Guard. But later, when I died, I took over his body from him."

"What!" Dral stared blankly.

"I was killed on Earth when an invasion came from a planet called Zanji," Quorne continued. "At that time a being named Kron was ruling the destiny of Earth, and it was by him that I was slain. But death does not bring oblivion of the mind. Upon the death of my body, my mind was free, of course. It had only one objective, to assume again a material form as nearly approaching the dead one as possible. Imagine my surprise when I found a body identical—here, on this world! I took it over, blasting out the weak mind of the creature ruling it, and I have used this body ever since. I can hardly believe that I ever died, so completely does this body duplicate the original the one I possessed."

"You blasted the 'weak' mind of the original captain of the guard," Dral said. "I would not call any of our race weak. We are masters of thought processes, otherwise we could not have duplicated the bodies of the far distant people of Earth."

"I admit you understand the rudiments of thought processes, and that you are far ahead of natural Earth people in development," Quorne responded, "but you are not ahead of me. I am more intelligent than you. Jupiter was my first home, my birthplace, and I was once adviser to Abna, himself a towering peak of intellect. So, ranged against Abna, the brilliant Golden Amazon, the adroit Viona—who was married to me when I had my own body on Earth—and myself, you stand little chance of succeeding in the plan of conquest you have devised."

"But I have no plan of conquest!" Dral protested, and then looked away as the relentless heliotrope eyes pinned him.

"You lie," Quorne stated flatly. "Long ago I read your mind, and I know exactly what you aim to do. You told the Amazon, Abna, and Viona that you only duplicated yourselves as Earth people so that you could have physical vestment instead of clumsy bacterial bodies. That was a lie. Your real aim is the bloodless conquest of every planet in the System by means of physical transposition. You plan first to conquer Earth by duplicating here among yourselves everybody who exists on Earth—then later you intend to put the counterfeit bodies on Earth and bring the originals here by scientific dissembly processes. The counterfeits would be your own people, obeying your orders, and on Earth nobody would know that the switch had been made."

Dral was silent, plainly disturbed.

"Altogether," Quorne commented, "a highly ingenious plan, with no Earthling guessing that his neighbor, or even a member of his family, might be an enemy in disguise."

"Presumably you have read my thoughts," Dral said. "That being so, I am glad that you approve. Tell me, though, who were you when on Earth?"

"My name is Sefner Quorne, and before the death of my former body, my ambition was nothing less than the ultimate conquest of the Universe—in which I was always balked by the Golden Amazon and her contemporaries. Now that I again have a body, my ambition remains unaltered, the only difference being that you have greatly simplified matters."

"We shall operate as we see fit, Quorne," Dral said.

"I think not." Quorne smiled acidly. "The greater intelligence always dominates. I am greater than you, therefore you will do as I say. This scheme you have devised for bloodless conquest will be put into effect, certainly, but under my direction. You stand no chance against the Golden Amazon, Abna, Viona, and myself, but if you range yourself on my side, we can probably succeed in mastering the Universe."

"By replacing Earthlings with counterfeits?"

"Exactly. Afterwards, when enough of your race have patterned themselves after the fashion of Earth people, we will transfer the original Earth people here and switch the counterfeits in their place. That is simple enough by atomic dissembly. The bodies are reduced to their atomic components, transmitted to wherever necessary, and there reassembled. The Amazon herself created that System, and a very brilliant one it is."

"And if I refuse to work with you, Quorne?"

"You will go down to everlasting defeat. Since I am capable of reading your thoughts, you can never make a move without my knowing it. So, obviously, you had better come to terms."

Dral was silent, realizing that he was beaten.

"It is also to our benefit," Quorne continued, "that we have on this counterfeit world the duplicated images of the Amazon, Viona, and Abna. They will be extremely useful to us. The originals must be brought here at a later date and held captive by every known method. Once that is done, conquest will be simple."

Dral gave a shrug. "Very well, Quorne, since I am powerless to defy you, I have no alternative but to work with you—"

CHAPTER TWO
PLAN IS EXPOSED

The young woman who made her way up the driveway of the huge modern residence in outer London was obviously nervous, behaving very much like a trespasser in forbidden territory. And with good reason. The London home of the Golden Amazon had all the appearance of a scientific house of mysteries, from the strange aerials atop the lofty roof to the many laboratory annexes attached to the house. Even along the driveway there were curious instruments embedded in metal pillars, some of them emanating strange but harmless rays of pink and blue light. Not being a scientist, the young woman could not guess the reason for such apparatus; and she certainly did not realize that her movement up the drive was being reproduced on a screen in the Golden Amazon's laboratory, and that the sound of her timid footsteps was audible in loudspeakers.

The young woman reached the massive metal front door, but before she had a chance to ring the curiously fashioned bell, the door opened silently and revealed an expanse of tastefully furnished hall illumined with the beams of the March evening sunlight.

"Please go into the lounge on your right," a voice said from a concealed loudspeaker. "I will be with you in a moment."

The girl gave an awed glance about her and then resumed her uncertain advance. Entering the huge lounge she surveyed its opulence and magnificent modern appointments—then cold-light globes glowed into being.

The young woman sank into an armchair, gazing at an astonishing clock high in the wall that registered even days, months, and years and made no sound. She was thankful to have got this far without mishap. Her friends had warned her that to try to invade the home of the Golden Amazon was to risk death.

"Good evening."

The girl jumped out of her chair, suddenly aware of the tall, supple woman who had entered the room. She moved with the grace of a tigress and the poise of an empress, clad in a sweeping blue gown, which, falling from her smooth shoulders, revealed the deep satin gold of her skin and the steel-hard muscles that rolled softly with every movement she made.

"I'm Elsa Vincent, a machine-operator in the city," the girl said. "I know I have no right to question such a woman as you, Miss Brant, but— You are Miss Brant, of course? The Golden Amazon?"

"Yes." The Golden Amazon inclined her head and waited.

The young woman sat down again, staring. She had

to admit the incredible beauty of the woman facing her. Proud arrogance and high intelligence were moulded into those perfect features and violet eyes. And there was nowhere a line or crease of age, even though it was generally conceded that Violet Ray Brant, the Golden Amazon, must be well over sixty years of age. Here was eternal youth and magical loveliness, crowned with a wealth of rippling golden hair that set off the enormous rubies holding it back from her high, wide forehead.

"You said your name is Elsa Vincent," the Amazon prompted. "Can I help you in some way?"

"Yes, but—I haven't much money Miss Brant, to pay for your advice and—"

"Money does not concern me, Miss Vincent, if the problem is scientific. What is the trouble?"

"Do you believe the dead can return?" the girl asked surprisingly.

The Amazon seated herself, studying the city girl curiously.

"Scientifically, yes," she replied. "In the normal course of events—definitely no."

Elsa Vincent hurried on. "Three days ago my young man, chosen for me by the Eugenics Bureau, was killed in a machine accident. I went with his family to the funeral. But tonight he walked into the house as though nothing had happened and suggested we go out for the evening. He made no reference to his death, or anything. I simply panicked for a while and rushed to tell his family. They couldn't understand it, either, so

I said I'd see you. They warned me that a woman so high in affairs as you would never bother with me, but I risked it."

"It is certainly unique," the Amazon mused. "And what has this young man to say about it?"

"He seemed taken aback when I told him he had been killed and buried; then he laughed it off and said it must have been a case of mistaken identity."

"Obviously, then," the Amazon said, "the thing to do is have the corpse which was buried exhumed and examined."

Elsa Vincent said uneasily: "Yes, I suppose so, but I hardly think the authorities would believe such a story."

"Tell me," the Amazon said, "are you convinced this young man is the young man you have always known? He is not different in any way?"

"Not physically. But his memory seems a bit hazy. I referred to one or two matters when he came to my home, but he seemed to have to struggle to remember them."

The Amazon said: "For every scientific problem there is always a solution. What is this young man's registration number?"

"78965 LH."

The Amazon registered it in her mind and then nodded. "Thank you, Miss Vincent. I would suggest you carry on, if you can, as though nothing had happened and leave the rest of the details to me. I'll discover the explanation."

Elsa Vincent smiled in relief as she rose. "Yes, I

believe you, Miss Brant, but I'm going to find it hard to carry on as though nothing had happened."

To this the Amazon made no comment. She saw the girl to the outdoors again, then she turned and hurried through to the main laboratory. A gigantic, blond-headed man in protective suiting glanced up inquiringly as she appeared and stopped the electronic machine he was experimentally operating. A slim girl, likewise in protective suiting with copper-gold hair and bright blue eyes, emerged from the midst of an electrical apparatus.

"Well?" asked Abna, unfastening his suiting. "What did she want?"

"An explanation as to why her dead fiancé should suddenly walk into the house as though nothing had happened."

"That all?" Viona asked, with her bright smile. "I am surprised you took up time bothering with her, mother—especially while this atomic experiment is on hand."

"The scientific mystery to which I will not pay attention has yet to appear," the Amazon replied, and gave the details of the interview. When she had finished, Abna and Viona were obviously puzzled.

"It must be mistaken identity," Viona declared. "It can't be anything else."

"I hope it isn't," the Amazon answered ambiguously, and turned to the visiphone. In a moment or so she had been automatically contacted by the private beam with government headquarters. The moment she appeared on the screen at the other end respect came into the speaker's voice.

"Yes, Miss Brant? At your service."

"Three days ago," the Amazon said, "a worker with registration number 78965 LH was buried, following his death in a machine room. I require the corpse exhumed and its image televised to me. The matter is urgent."

There was no suggestion of argument since the word of the Golden Amazon was law. "Very well, Miss Brant; we'll attend to it immediately. Do you wish to add details as to why you have made this request?"

"Not yet, but I may do so later. Thank you."

The Amazon switched off and stood thinking. Vaguely surprised at her preoccupation Abna strolled over to her.

"I'm puzzled, Vi," he confessed. "I don't want to take the effort to read your thoughts, so why not tell me why such a trifling problem as this interests you?"

"I, too, would like to know," Viona put in.

"It interests me because of its implications," the Amazon replied. "If what I am thinking proves correct, it will be found that there is no corpse in the grave."

"What!" Viona exclaimed, startled. "Then he has genuinely come back from the dead?"

"No; not quite that." The Amazon turned away, obviously unwilling to discuss the matter further until she had all the facts. "Let us see what develops first. In the meantime we have routine science to attend to."

Viona glanced at her father, then shrugged. Had he

wished, he could quite easily have read the Amazon's mind, but unless extreme emergency demanded otherwise, he always respected her privacy.

For perhaps an hour, normal laboratory work—research into atomic laws—continued, then came the call for which the Amazon was waiting. She picked up the visiphone as it buzzed and the face of the government official appeared on the scanner.

"Examination of the coffin of Worker 78965 LH reveals the coffin to be empty, Miss Brant." There was a wondering look in the man's eyes. "How this comes to be the case it is hard to understand, for the screws on the coffin lid were still in place."

"Thank you," the Amazon said, a gleam in her violet eyes. "That is all I wished to know."

"It is? But is it the correct answer?"

"As far as I am concerned it is, yes. I am much obliged."

The Amazon switched off and found Abna and Viona gazing at her. They had heard the official's voice in the receiver.

"Any suggestions?" Abna asked.

"Yes." The Amazon tightened her mouth. "Just one—Neptune!"

Abna looked puzzled and then sighed. "Well, I suppose I ought to see the connection, Vi, but I don't."

"Purely because you're not exerting yourself," she replied sharply. "Think, Abna! You have the powers of a god when you care to use them—but how rarely you do!"

"What's all this about Neptune?"

"Well, you surely haven't forgotten that we discovered Neptune, or at least part of it, to be a duplicate of Earth? Even to containing people who look like Earthlings?"

"No, I haven't forgotten, but— Wait!" Suddenly Abna got a grip on the situation. "Are you suggesting that this worker is a Neptunian?"

"I am. The whole business seems pretty plain to me. The Neptunians—or rather the Uranians, since they have migrated from Uranus—have started sending their doubles here, at the same time removing the originals."

"What!" Viona exclaimed. "But—but at that rate what's going to happen? Nobody's going to know who is genuine and who isn't."

"Exactly. It is also perfectly logical, from this premise, that the Neptunians are bent on conquest. Plainly they must use an atomic dissembler to accomplish their purpose. A counterfeit Earthling is sent there, garbed exactly like the Earth original, and the Earth original is switched back to Neptune. But in this one instance there has been a mistake."

"And a big one—for them," Abma said grimly. "They were not aware that this worker had died in the interval since they took his original pattern—but they will be now, because the exchange will hand them a corpse. Possibly they will even realize that they have unwittingly exposed their hand."

"Possibly," the Amazon admitted.

"The lapses of memory are plainly accounted for then," Viona commented. "A Neptunian, sent here, would be versed in the life of his original counterpart, of course, but there might be some things he wouldn't know, things which even radio waves and television cannot tell to the watchers of Neptune."

CHAPTER THREE
TOO LATE TO ACT

Abna said: "Hundreds of Neptunians may be in our midst and no normal people are aware of it."

"Quite likely." The Amazon moved restlessly. "Thank heaven that girl brought this to our notice, otherwise months might have elapsed before we found out the deception. Not that any of this is any surprise to me. You remember my saying when we escaped from Neptune, that the last thing I could believe was that the Neptunians were engaged in making themselves resemble Earthlings purely for the sake of it? Not they! Why, there are even duplicates of ourselves on Neptune, the very duplicates which enabled us to make our escape."

The Amazon's violet eyes met Abna's. At that instant the same thought had struck both of them.

"Quorne!" the Amazon exclaimed.

"Yes," Abna conceded, reflecting. "That guard we defeated when we escaped looked identical to him. Yet the original Quorne is dead."

"So we believe," the Amazon mused. "But—" She stopped, lost in speculation.

"Would one of you mind telling me what this is all about?" Viona pleaded. "What is there about this man named Sefner Quorne which always seems to trouble you? I've heard you mention him so often, and always in the terms of healthy respect."

The Amazon hesitated and gave Abna a glance. Though she no longer remembered the fact, Viona had once been the wife of the original Sefner Quorne and by him had had a son, Sefian. The child's mathematical genius, at the age of two years, had saved the Universe from destruction, but since that very conquest had involved the death of the son and produced disastrous bereavement upon Viona, Abna had blotted from her mind all memory of her son and Quorne. But she was always dimly aware that, somewhere, a piece was missing from her life.

"Quorne," Abna said, "was my adviser on Jupiter, Viona, long before you were born. More than once he has tried to master the Solar System with his superb science, and each time your mother and I have beaten him. The last we heard of him, when the Dark threatened to engulf the Universe, was that he had been killed—by a being of another world named Kron. But on Neptune, when we escaped from there, there was an individual heading the guard who looked exactly like him. A man with purple eyes and jet-black hair. If he really was Quorne, reincarnated, then we can be pretty sure that this Neptune counterfeit business has his mind back of it."

"Meaning," Viona asked, "that this is yet another

effort on his part to wrest power?" Then, as her father nodded, she laughed contemptuously. "And is he fool enough to think he can stand up to us three? Why, between us, we can—"

She stopped. Something was different about the laboratory. She and her mother and father noticed it at the same moment. It was hazing strangely under the force of electromagnetic stresses. Then all three of them cried out helplessly as unendurable anguish descended upon them and they were snuffed into oblivion.

Gradually the blankness of total unconsciousness lifted. Minds and then bodies knitted themselves swiftly back into place. Unhurt, but utterly bewildered, the Amazon, Abna, and Viona stood gazing before them—once again at a laboratory, but certainly not their own. What appeared to be Earthmen were grouped around a massive switch-panel, the foremost being slender in build, remarkable for his high forehead, polished black hair, and heliotrope eyes,

"Quorne!" the Amazon exclaimed.

"A most successful transit," Quorne commented, smiling tautly as he came forward. "I assume that I have no need to explain to such distinguished scientists as yourselves what has happened?"

"Presumably," Abna retorted, "you have transferred us from Earth to here—Neptune—by the process of atomic dissembly, our bodies being broken down into atomic aggregates and then reassembled here?"

"Exactly," Quorne agreed. "But there is another ramification. At the moment of departure from Earth you were replaced by exact counterparts, in identical clothing. Observe."

He gave an imperious signal and in response two of the men at the switch-panel became active. The laboratory lights dimmed somewhat and upon a screen there appeared another laboratory, the one which the Amazon, Abna, and Viona had formerly been occupying. Now they intently watched what appeared to be themselves looking about them in wonder.

"Your counterparts," Quorne explained dryly, as the lights came up again. "But only in appearance. Their minds, as you have good reason to know, are of a very low order, as is their physical strength."

"I suppose," the Amazon said, "that those are the three whom we used as decoys when we escaped captivity here?"

"Exactly. I leave it to you to imagine the effect when those three duplicates of yourselves are ranged on my side on Earth. The people will have nobody to turn to. They will be at the mercy of what they think are four of the greatest scientists ever known—the truth being, of course, one scientist and three dummies who will do exactly as I tell them."

"Would it be asking too much to inquire how you come to be alive after Kron of Zanji killed you?" the Amazon asked.

"You are acquainted with the boundless abilities of mind, Miss Brant, so the solution should have occurred to that able brain of yours. If you found your body destroyed and your mind free—and then discovered an identical body—what would you do?"

"Take possession, granting the other mind was weaker than mine."

"In my case it was," Quorne said. Then his eyes went to Viona. "My wife does not seem to have much to say," he commented.

Viona looked at him. "Are you referring to me?" she demanded. "I'm not your wife, and never will be."

"Not very convincing," Quorne replied acidly. "What became of Sefian, our son, who was going to do so much?"

"I can only assume," Viona replied, "that you are completely insane."

It was Quorne's turn to look puzzled. He concentrated for a moment and then frowned. "Very strange. In her mind I read no recollection of me at all, and even less of Sefian."

"Sefian died destroying the Dark which threatened to overwhelm the Universe," Abna replied. "Viona does not remember that happening, any more than she remembers Sefian. You, too, are obliterated in her thoughts."

The purple eyes sharpened. "In other words, Abna, you used that mind of yours to blot out her memory of me?"

"I did. And her mind must be the sweeter for it."

Quorne tightened his thin mouth for a moment and then he relaxed. "Oh, very well. Since the original Quorne's body died, I suppose the claim is no longer valid. Not that it signifies now in any case. I have far more things to do than concern myself over Viona."

Viona gave a bewildered look but did not say anything. The conversation had sailed far above her head.

"With your arrival here," Quorne said, "my plans are ready for action. You will have gathered that these people of Neptune, intelligent though they are, are entirely under my dictates? Including Dral, the leader of the state. I intend to return to Earth and there, with your duplicates, seize the power I've so long striven for. After that will come Mars—again by counterfeit work, our agents being mixed unidentifiably with the originals so that they cannot be detected. You three will stay here—and unlike the last time there will be no escape. I would kill you, but I may have need of your scientific knowledge someday."

"And you think we'd give it?" Abna asked in contempt.

"That would depend upon the process used to extract it.... For the moment, I have explained all that is necessary."

"Except the blundering mistake you made in sending the living counterfeit of a dead man among your latest batch of transferences," the Amazon commented, watching the slowly advancing guards narrowly.

"Yes." Quorne looked bitter for a moment. "That was the fault of these idiots with whom I'm working. We have telescopic and radio powers sufficient to identify and study every living soul on earth, but on that particular occasion no second check-up was made of the person concerned, with the inevitable result that we received a corpse and sent a live man. I guessed you might look into the matter and, when I came to study you across space, I saw that was just what you were doing. Before you could act I brought you here, and here you will stay. Take them away," he added, turning to the guards.

Though she knew escape was impossible, the Amazon's fury spilled over. As the two nearest guards came to seize her, she lashed out with her fists. They howled in anguish as her knuckles smashed their jaws and sent them spinning backwards.

The other guards hesitated, but before they could drag out their guns Abna and Viona were upon them, each using their superhuman strength to wipe out a little score they owed. Quorne turned to the switch panel and moved a button. A slide shot up in the wall, and as the Amazon finished overpowering the last guard, she swung to look at six massive metal robots advancing with pincer-hands extended.

She waited until they were almost upon her and then slammed her bunched fist into the grille that formed the 'stomach' of the nearest creature. But her fingers were trapped in steel claws and all her frantic efforts failed to budge them. By the time Abna and Viona had hurried to her aid, it was too late.

Quorne moved over to the robot that was imprisoning the Amazon's hand and made adjustments on its switch controls. Wincing, she pulled out her torn fingers as the steel grip relaxed.

"My apologies," Quorne murmured cynically. "You have only yourself to thank for your condition, Amazon."

The Amazon did not answer. She watched her hand swiftly restore itself to normal under the influence of Abna's mental powers. Quorne studied the phenomenon with interest and then shrugged.

"A pity you do not turn such mental power to better uses, Abna," he remarked. "You could master the universe if you wished."

"I don't wish," Abna snapped. "I leave grandiose dreams like that to misguided intellectuals like yourself."

Quorne turned away, and his mental orders reacted on the sensitive receiving apparatus of the robots to the extent of getting them on the move with the hapless trio in their midst. Unable to help themselves, they were taken from the laboratory and down the corridor outside, then in an elevator to the lowest depths of the building. Here in this subterranean space there was dim lighting and rows of barred metal doors, obviously dungeons.

But no ordinary cell had been prepared for the three. It was apart from the others, in the opposite wall, its door composed of solid metal except for ventilation holes at the top. In front of it, only waiting to be slid into position on a special wheeled platform, was a block of stone about ten feet square.

CHAPTER FOUR
THE BIG BREAK

The Amazon submitted to being half-thrown into the cell by the robots, Abna and Viona stumbling in after her. Then the door slammed shut, was electrically locked, and finally there came a heavy bump as the big stone was pushed into position.

"Do you suppose they intend to leave us here?" Viona asked presently, looking around her upon the metal walls, faintly visible in the dim light from the ceiling.

"I suppose so, until Quorne decides what comes next," Abna replied. "We shan't be left to die, since I gather he is hoping to use us in the future. In the meantime, since I have a distinct dislike for such complete confinement, I had better see how we can get out."

The walls were composed of solid sheets of metal without any sign of joining. The ceiling was similar, a solitary lamp glowing in its centre. Above again, presumably, was the whole mass of the building. The only opening was in the ventilator grille at the top of the door, which the stone outside left clear.

"Even if we could smash open that grille we'd be no

better off," Abna said. "It would be too small for us to get through. And we have no weapons with us."

The Amazon said: "I had just changed for dinner when Elsa Vincent arrived."

Viona said: "Somebody is bound to come and feed us, and they can't do it except by opening the door and pushing back the stone. We might do something then."

"I think not," came the voice of Sefner Quorne, apparently from the air itself. "I am aware of your conversation, but do not trouble to discover the loudspeaker from which my voice is emanating. There is no loudspeaker: it is a transmission to you direct, and your brains are capable of picking it up. Nobody will open the door until I am ready for them to do so. As for food, it will reach you like this."

There was a pause, then out of the air itself there materialized a tray filled with quite a sizeable meal and costly essences. There came a dry chuckle from Sefner Quorne as the tray finally settled on the floor.

"The fourth dimension can be most useful at times," he said. "Now I must leave you. I have much to do on Earth. We shall meet upon my return, and when that happens, I shall have partly achieved my ambition to dominate the System."

His voice ceased and Abna clenched his fists in fury. Swinging around, he went to the door, locked his fingers in the grille, and pulled with all his colossal strength. But the metal was proof against him. He finally desisted and returned to the centre of the cell, where the Amazon and Viona were calmly partaking of a meal.

The Amazon whispered: "I can never understand why, when you have transcending powers, you never use them in a crisis!"

Abna said: "I prefer to be human and have some happiness."

The Amazon mused. "I've wondered many a time— However, in regard to our present problem, the answer is to think our way out."

"I have been trying to do that ever since we got in here!"

"I mean it literally," the Amazon said, pouring herself a glass of restorative.

"You mean," Viona asked, after a moment, "that we should break this prison down by mind force? That's asking a lot, mother, isn't it?"

"I don't think so—providing your father chooses to use the powers he possesses to the utmost degree. Matter is always subordinate to mind, so with his mind and my own—and yours, my dear—I do not see why we can't get free. We might as well make the attempt, because we'll certainly never escape by physical means, not this time."

"And when we have escaped?" Abna asked, eating slowly, and it was curious to note that he did not entertain any doubt that escape was possible. "What then? We shall only walk right into the hands of the Neptunians!"

"There you go again!" the Amazon exclaimed, irritated. "One moment you admit the possibility of getting out of this prison, and the next you ask how we fare amongst the Neptunians! We destroy them, of course, if they get in our way, and we'll use physical or mental means to do it, whichever is the more favourable."

"Physically we have no weapons beyond our strength, Vi, and that wouldn't be equal to an army of them. Neither would mental power. Destroying dead metal and stone is not difficult because there is no mental opposition—as I found on Saturn when I created the city of Millennia by thought alone—but when you deal with thinking beings there's a terrific amount of opposition."

"Only thing to do with that is deal with it when we come to it," Viona said. "For my part, I'm willing to try mother's suggestion."

Abna considered while he finished his meal, then nodded.

"Very well, we'll try it," he assented, "but let us have some order in the situation. We want particularly to know where the spaceport is located, so we can steal a machine and make good use of our liberty. We're considerably helped by the fact that this city is a duplicate of London, so once we know in which direction the spaceport lies, the rest is easy. Now, let me see what I can do."

He stood motionless, concentrating, and neither the Amazon nor Viona disturbed him, chiefly because they were incapable of reaching the heights of mental exaltation that were natural to him. For his own part, his mind objectified every detail that lay outside the prison cell, as clearly as though he was viewing it on a television screen.

"The spaceport lies that way," he said finally, pointing left. "That's the direction we have to go when we get out of here."

"A moment," the Amazon put in. "Why try and escape into space? Would it not be better to try to get to the dissembly equipment, which we know is above us in the laboratory in this very building, and then transfer ourselves back to Earth before Quorne gets there? Unless, of course, he has also used that method to cover the journey. It would be infinitely quicker, and we could get to grips with him much more swiftly."

Abna nodded. "Good idea. The spaceport notion we can use as second best. Now, are you ready?"

Viona, and the Amazon closed their eyes and began to concentrate their mind force against the solid metal and stone that hemmed them in. Abna, far more experienced in the art of mind control, kept his eyes open, but the rigidity of his body showed the immense concentrated effort he was making.

Gradually the unrelenting effect of the mind-waves began to make itself evident. The wall on the door side of the cell visibly misted until it was no more than a gossamer veil, its very atoms obeying the superior law battering at it.

"Come," Abna murmured in a faraway voice, and with the Amazon on one side of him and Viona on the other he stepped forward, entirely fearless, and kept on walking until they were in the midst of the hazy transparency. Here they needed the ultimate of unwavering concentration, for a fraction of a second's disbelief in their power would have snapped the wall back to normal, crushing them to atomic dust in the process. But no such thing happened. Beyond a faint tingling sensation, the radiant effect of atomic clusters in subjection to mind-force, they passed through the wall safely and found themselves in the dim corridor.

At that they relaxed and the wall reformed, as solid as before. Abna glanced about him but there was nobody in sight.

"So far so good," he commented. "Be ready for anything. We know our way back to the laboratory anyhow. If robots are about, ignore them and they will probably ignore us, since no minds will be directing them to watch us."

He started forward, Viona beside him, both of them regretful that they had no physical weapons they could use. They knew their limitations when it came to mental force.

Without mishap they mounted a flight of stairs to the upper corridor and then paused. Three men were approaching, looking exactly like Earthmen, and were obviously coming from the laboratory.

"One of them is Dral," Abna murmured to the Amazon. "You remember? We talked with him on the last occasion we were here? He's the ruler of the planet. From what I can read of his mind, he has just been into the laboratory to see Quorne off on his journey to Earth."

The advancing Dral and his two advisers stopped, utterly bewildered at the sight of the trio, then their hands flew to their guns. But in that instant they were overpowered.

The Amazon singled out Dral for herself, whirled him around, then delivered a blow that knocked him spinning backwards towards the corridor's huge window, outside which blazed the glare of the artificial sun. Dral gasped and choked, trying to recover himself, but before he could do so the Amazon was upon him again, her yellow fingers tight about his neck. To her surprise, however, she found her strength was unequal to the task of squeezing the life out of the ruler: in fact, she herself was gradually being overpowered as his hands clutched her throat and tightened relentlessly.

Encumbered as she was by her sweeping gown, she took the only chance she could and wrenched herself free, narrowly missing the savage jet of a flame gun which one of the other men fired at her. Neither Abna nor Viona had overpowered their own adversaries, either, and were glancing about them for a means of escape.

The Amazon hesitated no longer. Since the men seemed too tough to be smashed down by ordinary methods, the only thing to do was get them out of the way for a while. So she twisted backwards quickly, seized Dral by the collar and belt of his jacket, then whirled him over her head and through the big window. With a tinkling of glass he sailed outside, dropping down forty feet to the street below. In a matter of seconds

Viona and Abna had dealt likewise with the other two men, dodging the ray-gun beams that stabbed at them.

They sped down the corridor and into the laboratory. The place was deserted and the equipment switched off. Presumably Quorne had transmitted himself to Earth and the technicians had departed. Quickly the Amazon hurried to the dissembler and studied its panels, then she nodded in satisfaction.

"Practically a duplicate of my own invention," she said. "And the settings are registering Earth—for Quorne, I suppose—so we'll have no troubles in that direction. Quickly, one of you, switch on the power."

Viona obeyed, or attempted to, but before she could grip the master-switch a robot glided unexpectedly from its concealed recess and seized her arm with its pincer hand. Instantly she tried to use the other hand, but this, too, was prevented.

Abna glanced around and saw what was happening. Immediately he hurtled for the monstrosity of metal, and by sheer strength tore open the pincers holding Viona's arms. But by the time he had done this, other robots came gliding into view, evidently directed by post-hypnotic orders to protect the laboratory against all intruders.

"Get away from them!" the Amazon cried, and they all raced through the laboratory door into the corridor. They kept going until the corridor took a sharp right turn to the main street outside. In the doorway were guards, one on each side, guns at the ready. As the trio came hurtling towards them they swung, ready for action.

"Risk knocking them over," Abna said. "Quorne likely left orders for us to be left unharmed, so we'll hope they won't fire."

His guess was correct, and by the time the guards had been reached, their hands were wavering uncertainly about their guns—and that was as far as they got. Knuckles smashed into their faces and sent them reeling down the steps to the street. Passers-by, exactly akin to Earthlings, paused in amazement and helped the guards to rise.

CHAPTER FIVE
READY FOR ACTION

The Amazon, Abna, and Viona ran down the steps and darted off to the left, heading in the direction of the spaceport. Glances of amazement were cast after them, but since their attire was Earthly enough, even though they themselves looked far too magnificent to have ever been born on that planet, no more attention was paid to them. As they went they glanced back towards the high window through which they had flung Dral and his advisers and wondered if they had yet been found or whether the drop had killed them. Possibly not, since they had proven so hard to incapacitate.

"Ahead there," Abna exclaimed, dodging through the main street traffic in the blaze of the synthetic sun. "There's the air and space port, exactly as it would be positioned on Earth."

They gained the gateway of the spaceport and sped across the open area toward a group of space machines.

"Trouble coming," Viona exclaimed, pointing to the administration building. "We've been seen."

Abna and the Amazon looked. Men were hurrying across the field shouting.

They put on an extra spurt, gained the nearest machine, and tumbled through the airlock. The Amazon slammed home the immensely thick door and sealed it, just as the yelling guards arrived. Abna activated the controls and the vessel lifted, hurtled skyward by the underjets.

The acceleration was terrific, holding all three motionless whilst it lasted, then the last barrier of the Neptunian atmosphere was hurdled and free space was reached. Abna cut off the power and relaxed for a while.

"Close, but we managed it," he smiled. "Only a matter of setting our course for Earth and risking Quorne when he spots us approaching."

Viona said, "Better take a look at the fuel gauge."

Abna turned and looked and his expression changed.

"Nearly empty," he muttered, startled. "Vi, we can't do it. We couldn't even get to Uranus with that fuel, let alone Earth. Constant velocity wouldn't help us, either, because we need fuel to direct ourselves away from counter-attractive bodies like Saturn and Jupiter."

Viona, looking out on to the endless immensities of space, gave a cry.

"Look! We're being followed—and overtaken, too."

The Amazon and Abna gazed through the port. Three space machines, moving at a stupendous velocity, were in hot pursuit.

"Something puzzles me," the Amazon said, frowning. "These Neptunian people seem to have tremendous, resistive strength, nearly as much as we do ourselves, otherwise they would never be able to stand up to that acceleration. And think of the trouble we had overpowering them."

"The answer's simple," Abna replied. "Basically, despite the Earth-being patterns they have assumed, they are bacteria, remember—the most indestructible form of life in existence. But this is no time for talking," he finished. "They're gaining. We'll have to use what precious fuel we have left to outdistance them."

"But we can't head Earthwards!" the Amazon exclaimed. "They are in the way and we'd use up our fuel in—"

"We're heading for Pluto," Abna decided, nodding through the port to the remote planet on the edge of the system. "That's our only chance."

With that he restored the power again, but since the machine was already flying at maximum velocity there was no apparent alteration in sensation and no acceleration drag. Only a feeling of weightlessness and the sight of those three pursuers steadily gaining.

"Something wrong here," the Amazon said. "Those vessels are smaller than ours and yet they move faster. That isn't logical. We can get more power out of this vessel if we want, Abna. Maybe you missed something on this control panel."

She turned her attention to it, studying it carefully, then she suddenly jabbed out her hand. Immediately there was a mighty jolt and with a surge that flattened her, gasping, to the floor, the space machine darted into infinity at an inconceivable velocity, leaving the pursuers receding into specks in a matter of seconds.

"What—what have you done?" Abna panted, hardly able to control the weight of his jaws.

"There was a booster," the Amazon gasped. "Second series of jets which you hadn't used. Our fuel is probably nearly gone, but we're free of those machines. They'll not be able to stand this velocity."

Abna realized that this terrific speed could not be allowed to continue. Fuel must be conserved to save the ship from crashing when Pluto was reached. He began moving, each effort stupendous, until his wavering hand came within reach of the booster. With a supreme effort he deactivated it, and the former sense of weightlessness returned. Thankfully he staggered upright and helped the Amazon and Viona to do the same. They looked out of the window and failed to detect any sign of the pursuers anywhere. In that hop they had devoured millions of miles and brought Pluto immeasurably nearer.

"Got rid of them anyway," the Amazon said in satisfaction. "And we're moving at a high velocity. Might as well cut off the power again, Abna. We'll keep at this speed in free space and save all our fuel for the landing."

Quickly Abna cut off the jets and then turned with a grim face. "I doubt if we'll have enough to cushion our fall," he said. "Have to hope for the best. Incidentally, when we get to Pluto what happens? There's no way back."

"That depends," the Amazon answered. "It might

be possible to send a message to Earth by the radio, providing Quorne doesn't intercept it, and get ourselves picked up. Or some lone traveler might—"

"Some lone traveler won't!" Viona declared. "No travellers ever go beyond Pluto, or even as far, if they can help it."

The Amazon said to Viona: "See if there are any provisions aboard. We can't all sustain ourselves by mental force alone as your father can in an emergency."

Viona came from the locker with several cartons of tabloid food and drink.

"Plenty here," she announced. "Seems enough in there to keep us going for months."

While they restored their strength with the concentrates, they were speculatively silent, weighing up chances for the future—and the more they considered the problem the more complicated it seemed to get. To the Amazon and Viona at least.

"Sending a radio message to Earth will not do," the Amazon decided. "Quorne would be sure to intercept it and we don't want him to know we've escaped—or rather we don't want him to know where we are. He'll learn of our escape from the Neptunians themselves, I suppose."

"It's possible that on Pluto we may find copper," Abna said. "That will do for our power plant here and see us safe."

"If we don't," Viona remarked, "there's nothing to stop you creating some, father. Or is there?"

"We'll see," he replied. "I've already done a good

deal of mental work in breaking down that prison cell, and at the moment I can't rise to the effort of doing any more."

Viona crossed to the port. "Pluto!" she exclaimed. "We're nearly upon it. We must have been moving at a terrific speed."

The ship jolted violently as the forward jets suddenly blasted forth, hurling their cushioning effect against the little planet now dragging with all its gravitating power. So rapidly had the journey been made, the slowing-up process had not been done quickly enough.

Through the port, as the trio stared through it, Pluto's black and rocky surface, utterly destitute in the weak sun and starlight, came looming out of the void.

The vessel struck the surface rocks with terrific violence and from outside came the cracking of plates and the snapping of supports. Gasping, unable to help themselves, the three cannoned into each other, or were flung into the softly padded walls. Then at last the topplings and turnings came to an abrupt end and they were able to slowly rise and consider the situation.

* * * * * * *

Far away on Earth, Sefner Quorne materialized—as the dissembler had been arranged that he should—in the laboratory from which the Amazon, Abna, and Viona had been snatched. When he had recovered from the tremendous physical strain occasioned by the transition, he looked at the three who had witnessed his coming—the three who exactly duplicated the

Amazon, Abna, and Viona in everything except intelligence and supernormal physical powers.

"You will be useful to me, my friends," Quorne told them, moving forward. "You know how to obey orders. I told you to await my coming and you have."

The three did not make any comment. "Our first move," Quorne said, "will be to take over the government of this planet, which should be a simple task with so many agents ready and waiting to act on my orders. We can accomplish that purpose from this laboratory. You will have gathered that it belongs—or at least did—to the Golden Amazon?"

"So we understood," agreed Amazon II, coming forward, and in every particular, even to the sweeping blue gown she wore, she resembled the superhuman woman from which she had patterned herself.

"Henceforth," Quorne continued, "this laboratory shall be our headquarters, because it is equipped with every known scientific device invented by the Amazon, Abna, or their daughter Viona. I planned that I would materialize here for that very reason. Let it be understood that I shall always refer to you by the names of your originals, and you will implicitly obey whatever orders I give you. Is that understood?"

The three nodded.

Quorne smiled in satisfaction.

"Splendid! I would warn you that we shall have a great deal of opposition to master, but the very fear of the people should give us the victory. Believing that the four greatest scientists in the Solar System are ranged against them, they will give in without a struggle."

"Might I ask where our originals are?" asked Abna II. "It would not be very pleasant to suddenly find them among us, destroying all our schemes."

"That can never happen," Quorne answered with assurance. "They are imprisoned securely, and will remain so until I decide otherwise."

Half an hour later the space radio buzzed and he was told about the escape of the three prisoners whom he had imagined were effectively incarcerated.

"Everything that could be done was done," came the reedy voice of Dral over the colossal distance of space. The communication was instantaneous, the radio waves being received fourth-dimensionally through the Amazon's special radio equipment. "I myself with two colleagues tried to stop them, but we failed and suffered injury."

"Where have they gone?" Quorne demanded. "Are they heading for Earth?"

"According to the patrols who pursued them, they flew to Pluto, and crashed there. They could hardly do much else, since there was very little fuel in the machine they stole."

"Are you sure they crashed?" Quorne insisted.

"Yes. Our patrols saw it happen telescopically and broke off the pursuit. Pluto is an utterly barren world, so there is no chance of those three getting back. And should they attempt it, we will intercept them. Probably they would have headed for Earth, but our patrols turned them in the opposite direction."

"And they escaped their prison by some means unknown?" Quorne asked bitterly.

"Yes. It is a complete mystery."

"Not to me. I warned you of the danger we face in having those three against us. Keep Pluto watched—or better still, send patrols to the planet to discover what has happened and report to me. This means I shall work now with the constant fear that I may find myself up against my most formidable foes at any moment."

"On Pluto they are as good as in prison!" Dral insisted. "They haven't enough fuel to return."

"A man like Abna does not rely on material fuel," Quorne retorted.

Impatiently he switched off and then glanced at the duplicate trio.

"Bad news," he said grimly—and since they had heard the communication over the speaker, they nodded silently.

"Nevertheless," Viona II said, "they are stranded a vast distance away on a world known to be nothing but dead rock, so our plans ought not to be interfered with."

"I hope not," Quorne muttered. "The trouble is that I cannot impress upon you people that Abna in particular—and even the Amazon sometimes—is capable of tremendous mental feats, which set distance and other deterrents at naught. However, it is time we went into action."

CHAPTER SIX
IMPORTANT DISCOVERY

They moved into the positions, he directed in front of the television transmitter. Then he sat down in their midst and switched on the apparatus. After a moment or two, on every live television screen in the world, there appeared a color image of the quartet, swamping all other visual transmission, and after another moment sound transmission, too, was blanketed as Quorne spoke, the carrier wave he generated swamping everything else.

"To those of you unfamiliar with our identities I will explain," he said. "You are seeing Sefner Quorne, who is now speaking, and also the Golden Amazon, Abna of Jupiter, and Viona. At one time or another Earth has been ruled by the Amazon and by me. In the recent invasion of Earth by the heavy men of Zanji I was slain, but thought processes returned me to life. Once I ruled Earth and was overthrown by the Amazon, who then retired into scientific meditation and left the government to normal Earth people, only offering her scientific advice when it was needed. Now we have all decided to throw in our lot together and, from this moment onwards, shall rule not only this planet but every planet in the System."

And on faraway Pluto the Amazon, Abna, and Viona looked at each other when in due course they heard these words through the space machine's radio equipment.

"It all has a familiar ring," Abna remarked grimly. "And Quorne is running true to his ideals and his plans. With our duplicates ranged on his side, there is nothing to stop him securing the mastery of Earth by sheer bluff—"

He broke off and listened as the speaker resumed.

"Some of you will not agree that we four should rule Earth and the System, but that is immaterial. Our agents are already at their appointed posts and know, upon this broadcast, to act according to instructions."

The Amazon reached out and switched off the apparatus. Her face was troubled.

"Somehow," she said, "we have to get away from this graveyard of a planet. I think the best thing we can do is look for copper outside."

"That's easy enough," Viona responded, "but what good will it do when we find it? The forepart of the machine is so battered that the rocket tubes are telescoped and useless. We can see that even from the port here. And we haven't the necessary equipment to effect a repair."

"True," the Amazon admitted, gazing out on to the barren scene, and for a while afterwards none of them spoke. They were too busy absorbing the utter hostility of Pluto, enigmatic little world of the System, so far from the sun that his illumination was no brighter than that of a full moon on Earth. Everywhere there were craters and rocks, growing up into low hills, black and merciless against the even deeper black of space with its powdering of everlasting stars.

"In a while we'll also run into more trouble," Viona continued, summing things up with the bland incon-sequence of youth. "We heard the radio say earlier that patrols were coming from Neptune to look for us. When they find we're not dead, they'll throw every-thing they've got at us, and we shan't be able to hit back, because there isn't a single weapon on this machine. Without fuel, without weapons, and the ship broken down, we're not exactly in a eheerful position, are we?"

"How you do chatter!" Abna commented, musing,

"Sorry," Viona apologized, "but I might just as well state the facts, mightn't I?"

"If the worst comes to the worst," the Amazon said, "your father is capable of creating some copper, or a new ship, or even of making repairs by mental process."

"Don't be too sure of that," Abna objected. "That business with the prison was one of the toughest mental feats I've taken on for a long time. Like all unexpected strains, a rest is demanded afterwards. Don't count on me for large mental activities for some days yet."

"Which means we just sit here and wait, for some-thing to happen," Viona sighed.

"Please be quiet for a moment!" Abna said, and in

some wonder Viona watched her father's concentrated expression as he looked through the port. The Amazon turned to look with him, but beheld nothing save the empty rock plateau and the distant range of low hills.

"Queer," Abna said at length, puzzled. "I was just seeing if I have enough mental strength to do anything to help and my thoughts came right back at me! Luckily they were not vindictive, otherwise I might have been knocked out by the impetus of my own thinking!"

"What?" the Amazon asked.

"Like a mirror," he explained. "Like being dazzled by swinging a beam of light on to a mirror and getting it reflected back to you. There's something odd about this planet and we must investigate. Viona, get the spacesuits."

This was not difficult to do, since spacesuits were standard equipment on any vessel of the void. Viona brought three from the locker, and within minutes she and her father and mother were ready to investigate outside. Abna went first through the pressure lock, helping the Amazon and Viona after him, then they began moving—he leading the way—across the twilight darkness of the plain, Neptune's green bulk looming high above them. So far there was no sign of the patrols that had been ordered to investigate.

"Pluto is a mystery planet," came Abna's voice, through the audiophone. "A tiny world compared to the giants it has for neighbors, a gravity not dissimilar to that of Earth, and no atmosphere whatever or any life. Yet there is a mysterious something about it which no other planet has."

"For instance?" the Amazon questioned, looking about her through her helmet-visor.

"This," Abna replied, and stopped. Viona and the Amazon paused beside him and discovered he was looking towards a depression in the rocky landscape. It had a peculiar glint in the star and sunlight, rather like that of polished copper. It lay on the side of a vast wall of rock—a concavity fully two miles in diameter and a considerable distance away.

"What is it?" the Amazon questioned.

"You have the power of transmitting your thoughts, Vi, when you wish," Abna responded. "Not with anything like the same force as mine, true, but you can produce a certain effect. Just think of something pleasant and look at that rock cavity at the same time. You, too, Viona—try it. You have similar powers."

The women did as they were told and then recoiled as though they had been struck a physical blow. Astonished, they looked at each other.

"It's something reflective to thought waves!" the Amazon exclaimed in astonishment. "Not only that: it amplifies them a thousandfold."

"Exactly—operative, I imagine, only if the thoughts strike it in a straight line, much the same as light must strike a mirror. I sensed it from the space machine, since the port looks directly toward this mysterious depression. One is safe enough if not concentrating directly upon it—otherwise the reflected impact of mind-waves is so stupendous as to be destructive."

"How did it get here?" Viona asked. "It can't be a natural formation, surely?"

"It could be, but I don't think it is," Abna responded. "Tracing back mentally, I can visualize a time when there lived on this world a race of highly trained mental physicists who used this area of reflective thought-wave material for various purposes. They created it and it has remained ever since, untouched by climatic conditions since Pluto lost its atmosphere long since—and also unharmed by the utter cold of pure space. Its origin does not matter. It is the use to which it can be put which counts. Come back to the ship and I'll explain what I mean."

They returned quickly, and once divested of their spacesuits, Abna motioned to the screwed-down chairs and the three settled themselves.

"We have here on Pluto a weapon of devastating power," he said, "depending on how ingeniously we use it. You are both aware that I can, without any material aid, create matter by thought vibration, and at fairly considerable distances. Consider then the effect of such a matter creation amplified by that rock depression! Suppose destructive thought waves were trained on Neptune, amplified by that rock depression. Imagine the effect!"

The Amazon's violet eyes gleamed. "Of course! Every Neptunian on the planet would be destroyed."

"Just so. The Neptunians are supporting Quorne because they have to. Bereft of that support, his plans will be in jeopardy because he will have no more duplicate Earth people to call on. It will mean determining by mathematics exactly when Pluto's reflective depression is straight in line with Neptune. It's a problem in angles. Also—"

"Just a moment," the Amazon interrupted. "Don't forget that on Neptune there are thousands of Earth people, those who have been brought in exchange for their doubles transplanted to Earth. We'd kill all of them as well."

Abna fell to thought, but his meditation was interrupted by Viona as she sat gazing through the port.

"The patrols!" she exclaimed, leaping up. "Here they come!"

Immediately the Amazon and Abna got to their feet and gazed into the black sky. A curving "S" of rocket exhaust from each of six machines showed where they were descending from the upper heights toward Pluto's surface.

"They've certainly covered the distance from Neptune at a colossal speed," Abna commented. "Probably they used automatic controls to do it and made themselves unconscious meanwhile. Which is an interesting point. Being bacteria people at root, these Neptunians will be nearly impossible to kill by material means—but they cannot withstand mental power—"

"The point is, what do we do now?" the Amazon asked impatiently. "They're almost upon us and we have no weapons."

"We have that reflective rock and we're going to use it. When they spot this derelict vessel of ours and descend to investigate, it will put them in a straight line with that depression. We cannot concentrate from here or we would get the impact of thought as well as them. We must get outside and concentrate from an angle."

The trio had just left the vessel in their spacesuits when searchlights concentrated on the lost machine and the patrol began to descend rapidly.

"Keep beside me," Abna murmured through his audiophone.

Since the searchlights were concentrated on the lost spaceship, there was no danger of them picking up the trio moving swiftly amid the rocks. When they had gained a tall spur with an overhanging lip, Abna halted and pointed.

"This should do," came his voice. "There's the rock depression over there. We are well to one side of it, but that won't stop our thought waves striking it. They'll be reflected at forty-five degrees, which will make them travel in a straight line toward the patrol. All three of us will concentrate when I give the word. The most effective destructive thought is that of death. Be ready. *Think of death!*"

CHAPTER SEVEN
STEP BY STEP

The six machines came sweeping down one after another to the plain, settling only a few yards from the derelict space flyer. The occupants of all six machines emerged in their spacesuits, and apparently held a conference. Then, in a body, numbering twenty in all, they began to move.

"Now!" Abna murmured, and simultaneously he, the Amazon, and Viona all turned their concentration to the rocky depression, staring at it fixedly across the distances and hurling toward it the most destructive thoughts of which they were capable.

The effect on the spacesuited men of Neptune was shattering. They stumbled, clapping their gloved hands to their helmets and reeling dizzily. Every man fell to the ground, writhing. Indeed, so terrific was the concentrated mental power hurled at them, four of their number vanished entirely, utterly dissolved. In ten seconds not a man remained moving, and none had got as far as the derelict machine.

Abna commented, relaxing: "We have stumbled upon one of the most frightful weapons ever devised,

Vi."

They set off across the rocky expanse, and before long had reached their victims. Behind the helmet visors were the dead faces of apparent Earthmen. Neptunian duplicates of Earth people. That they were dead was more than obvious.

"Which gives us six machines from which to choose," Abna remarked. "Our problem is solved, as far as getting away from here is concerned, but we have still to work out how to use this weapon of ours to the best advantage."

He led the way to the nearest patrol ship and before long he, the Amazon, and Viona were once more settled in chairs, the airlock securely fastened, considering the task which now lay before them.

"When these patrolmen fail to return or make a report, more may come," Viona remarked.

"If more come before we've departed they will share the fate of their predecessors," the Amazon answered. "However, to revert to our particular problem: we cannot destroy the Neptunians en masse for fear of wiping out many thousands of our own people as well. Another thing, even if we did wipe out everybody on Neptune, our own people included, it would lead Quorne to believe that we are alive. He'd know that nobody else could pull a stunt like that. Then our chance of surprising him would be gone. And that's the only way we'll ever get the mastery of him—by surprise."

"I think," Abna said slowly, pondering, "that the best

move we can make would be to assume the identities of those three who are our doubles, whom Quorne has beside him on Earth. If somehow we could take their place without him knowing it, we'd be able to smash him at any moment we chose."

"To do that requires a dissembly machine," the Amazon pointed out. "That means returning to Neptune and we just wouldn't stand a chance."

"There may be a way round that," Abna said. "Let us suppose that there is and work out our plan on that basis. When we replace our doubles on Earth, the doubles will automatically be transferred back to Neptune in our place. Suppose we could leave them with orders to wipe out the Neptunian race."

Viona remarked: "The doubles would not have the brains."

"They might be made to have," Abna answered.

The Amazon insisted: "We have to get back to Neptune and use a dissembler. How?"

This issue held Abna in thought for several moments, then at last he smiled. "Simple enough! We use a decoy. We use our rock reflector to create it. Something that will make most of the Neptunians desert their planet in a hurry, only returning when they believe danger has passed."

The Amazon looked irritated. "Abna, would you stop talking in riddles!"

"I am thinking of a ghost star," he explained. "They do exist, you know—an aggregation of light waves which have been round the Universe and return to their starting point, the star which originally created them having long since fallen into cosmic dust. If you recall, as far back as the days of Eddington, ghost stars were referred to, and sometimes mistaken for the real thing. My plan is to create a ghost star by mental fusion, and move it through space so that it seems to be heading for Neptune at a terrific pace. The Neptunians will believe it is the real thing—a runaway—and will make a hasty exodus. When they do that, we will land on Neptune and perform our transference act, keeping Neptune covered meanwhile in the glare of the ghost star, which will make the Neptunians think their planet is being destroyed by a celestial conflagration. With our departure to Earth, the ghost star will move on leaving Neptune untouched. The Neptunians will return, fully satisfied that the phenomenon was that of a ghost star, an occurrence not impossible in celestial mechanics, and possibly they will feel fools at having run away from a mirage."

"Quite brilliant," the Amazon admitted, somewhat grudgingly, "but I foresee difficulties. How do we keep the bogus ghost star in position, following a track, when we shall no longer be on Pluto to direct its movements by thought?"

"The whole business is a matter of mental mechanics," Abna replied. "We work out first in mathematics the position in space where the ghost star will be created, the position being determined by which direction the rock depression is facing. When that is done, our mental wave will create a gigantic circular mass of light waves. Further thought waves will give it an impulse and direct it in a pre-charted track from which it cannot swing aside. It will be a genuine ghost star once created, but as harmless as fresh air. Neptune's mass will attract it and probably hold it for a while, but the velocity of the ghost star will be greater than the mass attraction of Neptune, so after a while the ghost star will just continue on its way—and what becomes of it doesn't matter to us. It will sail on through the Universe eternally, no doubt. All else apart, we ought to create the greatest decoy ever devised."

"Yes, that seems clear enough," the Amazon agreed, though despite her intellect she had some difficulty in keeping up with Abna's godlike conceptions. "Now another point: our doubles will return when we go to Earth. What will the Neptunians think when they find those three on Neptune and—we trust—nobody else?"

"That," Abna confessed, "is a vital point—and one I overlooked."

"The simplest answer to that," Viona said, "is to bring our doubles here, to this planet—in this very ship if you like. I mean make the actual transfer from here instead of Neptune. Then they will be out of sight when the Neptunians return to their own world, and they'll also be close enough to the rock-depression to use it for mental work."

"Right!" Abna exclaimed, his eyes gleaming.

"Then we go to Neptune, get dissembly equipment, and bring it back here, using the ghost star as our cover and decoy?" the Amazon questioned.

"Just that."

"We'll need all our strength to do it, too! Dissembly apparatus is no featherweight."

"We'll manage it," Abna declared. "And we shall also need something else. We'll never see our doubles to give them orders, and even if we could, their minds—as Viona has remarked—would not possess the power to hurl forth the destructive mental force needed to annihilate every inhabitant on that planet. So while on Neptune we must take recording apparatus, the type used for recording thought-impressions. They can be run from normal atomic batteries, such as we have on this space machine. On those recorders we can leave our thoughts. Normal sound projectors, actuated to operate by photoelectric beams, will come into action when our doubles return, telling them how to use the projectors, and the recorded thoughts. Thus our thoughts will be hurled at Neptune, but we shall be on Earth."

The Amazon said, "I wonder I didn't think of it myself."

"All of which assumes our doubles will do as we ask," Viona commented. "They will surely resent the idea of destroying their own people won't they?"

"That, too, can be overcome," Abna responded. "Instead of ordinary sound projectors, we'll use hypnosis projectors, the type common to any advanced laboratory such as they have on Neptune. That will compel the doubles to do as we ask, whether they like it or not." Abna smiled in satisfaction. "That seems to cover every point. Now let us work out the necessary mathematics."

* * * * * * *

So, while Sefner Quorne easily gained the mastery of Earth and laid his plans for the conquest of Mars by similar "duplication" methods, using the hapless Earth people as pawns, in the wastes of a derelict planet the three most brilliant minds in the Solar System plotted and computed to encompass his downfall.

The computations that Abna had spoken of almost lightly were far more complicated than at first had been realized. Three days and nights of untiring, unflagging mental effort were demanded to work out the details, there being no advanced computers present to help with the task. But at the end of the time, though worn out through their endeavors and lack of rest, they were convinced that everything was in order. In two more days Pluto would be in the correct position for the hurling into space of the necessary mental waves to create a ghost star.

Everything was so designed that almost split-second timing was called for, even to the point of the three Earth doubles, when they arrived, having Neptune in the correct position to be affected by the waves coming from the rock-depression on Pluto. The only thing which could cause hindrance would be the slowness of the Neptunians in leaving their planet, or returning to it, and since this was the unknowable factor it had to be left to chance.

Exhausted by their labours, the three retired to rest in the space machine's bunks, leaving the alarm system in operation in case any fresh patrols should appear— but none did. At the end of thirty-six hours of solid sleep they awoke again, fully refreshed, and ready for the gigantic feat of mental science, which was the first stage in their plan.

CHAPTER EIGHT
TEMPORARY HALT

First they had a meal, listening to the space radio meanwhile. There were still twelve hours to, go before Pluto would be in the spatial position they wanted for their experiment.

From the radio it was evident that events on Earth were following an almost familiar pattern. In such scientific times invasions of Earth had become almost commonplace—but, for Earth people, the most frightening aspect of all was the fact that they were utterly without a defender. On all previous occasions the Golden Amazon, Abna, and Viona had fought on their side, but now—as it appeared—their champions had gone over to the ruthless enemy. They were utterly desolated and reduced to the level of slavery, working mainly for Quorne in the construction of the various machines and instruments he would need in his avowed conquest of the System and then the Universe.

"From the look of things," the Amazon said, switching off in disgust, "we are not going to have an easy struggle to regain our reputations. The people have us labelled as deserters."

"We'll soon change their minds when we destroy Quorne," Abna answered. They'll assume we have used some clever strategy and let it go at that."

"This time," the Amazon muttered, "let us make as reasonably sure as can be that Quorne is really wiped out, physically and mentally."

Abna said: "To ensure total destruction of the body is simple, Vi—but the mind is another problem entirely. However, let us face that problem when we come to it."

Viona said: "When the ghost-star is created and heads for Neptune, the Neptunians will depart—all of them, we hope—and we shall see them through the telescope on this machine; but how do we keep out of their sight in our journey to Neptune for the equipment we want?"

"We detour from here and approach Neptune from behind the ghost-star," Abna answered. "The star will hide us, for one thing, and for another, the Neptunians will obviously go away from it and not towards it. That answer the question?"

"Completely!"

"Now let us rehearse our plan," Abna said. "You, Vi, take charge of the light-wave concentration; you, Viona, concentrate upon the cosmic path; and I will devote myself to the initial effort of creating the right shape and size of light waves from space itself. Now let us rehearse and be sure of our timing."

So thorough were they that they kept at it for eight hours. The remaining four hours they spent in resting or discussing commonplaces; then when the time was nearly up, they took restoratives, donned their space-suits, and went outside, taking up positions a quarter of a mile from the queer area of reflective rock.

Abna studied the illuminated watch strapped over the wrist of his spacesuit, and then surveyed the utter black of the airless sky and its hosts of hurtfully bright stars. Far away to the approximate east of Pluto, Neptune was sailing in green splendour. Pluto having moved on in its orbit, the reflective rock area was now facing empty space, out towards the Milky Way—a superb place to create a ghost star.

"You have your minds ready?" Abna asked at length, and the gleaming helmets of the Amazon and Viona both nodded.

"And I have the distance fixed in my mind," Abna added. "The seconds are running out— Be ready for my signal. I will drop my hand."

Viona and the Amazon became completely motion-less, gazing towards the rock area. Abna raised his hand—then he lowered it and commenced the most amazing scientific attempt at creation every attempted. Three minds, each of them powerful beyond the ken of ordinary beings, worked in unison, controlling one particular formation of the united conception. To Abna belonged the initial task of determining distance and creating light-wave photons when the vast distance was covered. Travelling at the speed of thought, untrammelled by material laws, the creation was instantaneous. His thoughts, amplified many thousand -fold times, fled across the awful reaches of infinity, followed almost instantaneously by the thoughts of the Amazon and then Viona.

Breathless at their own audacity they waited—and then Abna gave an audible sigh. "We've done it—the ghost-star has been created in the deeps of interstellar space. It isn't visible yet in the normal way, but my mind can sense it. Now all we have to do is wait until its light-waves reach the rim of the solar system.

"In a few weeks," Abna added, "the Neptunians will realize their danger. Until then we can only wait—and watch—and thank the power that rules the cosmos that our scientific effort has proven successful."

* * * * * * *

Sefner Quorne was in the Amazon's laboratory, which he had taken over as his headquarters while ruling Earth, when Amazon II came in to him. Musing over a multitude of problems, he watched her approach. In every detail this magnificent woman was a replica of the superwoman—except in intelligence, and this showed in her violet eyes. They had none of the brilliant, even vengeful sparkle, of her ruthless original.

"Well, what is it?" Quorne asked impatiently. "I'm busy. The workers in the space machine factories are giving trouble and they'll have to be quelled. Tell Abna to see what he can do with them— And haven't you anything better to do than parade around preening yourself in your original's glory?"

Amazon II halted at the desk. "I—I thought I should tell you, Quorne, that something is wrong." Her voice, though identical to the Amazon's own, was hesitant.

"Wrong?" Quorne laughed shortly. "I'm aware of it! Far too many things! Getting absolute control of a planet full of resistant people is by no means easy—"

"No, not that. Something's wrong in space. I just noticed it when making a survey for the interstellar conquest you are planning. There's a star visible where it shouldn't be, and according to previous star-plates it is growing with tremendous rapidity."

"Growing!" Quorne sat up sharply. "You mean a runaway? But that is an extremely rare occurrence— are you sure?"

Amazon II shrugged. "Maybe so, but it's there."

He hurried from the room with Amazon II following him. The observatory was next to the laboratory and darkened at the moment to permit astronomical study—quite possible by day with the light-photon magnetizers with which the telescopic reflector was equipped.

Tight-lipped, Quorne looked into the mercuroid mirror of the instrument, his heliotrope eyes fixed on a plainly visible star of the first magnitude. Even as he watched it, it grew larger on the hairline scale drawn mathematically across the mirror.

"Let me see earlier photo plates," he ordered, without looking up and Amazon II went to the cabinet and handed them over. He studied them, his face becoming grimmer as he did so.

"I was right, wasn't I?" Amazon II asked, her beautiful face sourly resentful.

"Only too right," Quorne admitted. "That is definitely a runaway star and moving at a tremendous speed. The matter should have been reported to me much earlier. Contact Dral on Neptune immediately.... And where are Abna and Viona?" he asked, looking about him.

"Where you sent them," the double answered sullenly, turning to the radio equipment in the corner. "Or have you forgotten that you dispatched Abna to supervise the building of space machines, and Viona to take control of the laboratories?"

Quorne put down the plates and went across to Amazon II. Catching her arm he swung her round viciously, then he delivered a stinging slap across her face.

"That is to remind you that I am entitled to respect, and I mean to have it."

"And if the others or myself were to tell the people of this planet that we are not the real thing, what then?" the woman demanded angrily, holding her throbbing cheek. "You would not get very far, Sefner Quorne, would you?"

"Neither would you!" His eyes glinted. "One hint of the truth about yourselves, and I'd kill the lot of you and bluff out the story you had told."

Amazon II said no more, but the resentful look was back in her violet eyes. Turning to the radio equipment, she switched it on and, after an interval, Dral of Neptune was contacted. Immediately Quorne drew the microphone to him.

"Quorne speaking," he explained briefly. "Our star plates show a runaway approaching from the region of the First Galaxy moving at high speed. Please confirm if you have you any record of it—"

Dral's reply was instantaneous, thanks to the fourth dimensional set-up incorporated into the Amazon's radio equipment. "Yes—a very disturbing one," he responded. "That star is headed directly towards this planet. Our calculations show that it will strike us in approximately three Earth weeks. Our only course is to leave this planet as quickly as possible."

"But you can't!" Quorne protested when he heard the response. "That will ruin everything we're working for! I need you people as duplicates. My plans for the conquest of colonized Mars are almost complete."

"Our lives are more important than any conquest!" Dral countered. "The conquest will have to be abandoned, as far as we are concerned, at least. When that star strikes this world, everything upon it will be destroyed. I am now making preparations for exodus and was going to advise you."

Quorne said: "I want full details of this runaway. I have had no time yet to make my own calculations and I wish to find out how I stand. If Earth and the inner planets are also going to be affected, I shall have to postpone my operations."

"They will not be affected," Dral said. "The path of the runaway takes it across the outermost edge of the System, and this planet of ours has the misfortune to be directly in line. There will be perturbations, of course, with such a heavy body suddenly coming into the Solar System, but that can be tolerated. We propose returning to our native world until the cataclysm has passed, and if anything remains of this world after the star has gone on its way, we will retrieve it. We are leaving almost immediately before the first gravitational upheavals bring everything down on us. I am ending this transmission—now."

Quorne scowled on receiving Dral's final message. Evidently his mind was made up and he did not intend arguing any further.

"Does this mean an end of our plan of conquest?" Amazon II asked.

"No! Certainly not!" Quorne got to his feet. "For the time being, until the star has passed, we shall have to slow up our activities until we have determined the situation. That is the only difference. Continue the cosmic charting as before."

The woman nodded and turned back to her task and Quorne went back to the laboratory, his face taut.

Meanwhile, on Pluto the Amazon, Abna, and Viona were biding their time and taking readings of their cosmic creation at intervals. Since Pluto had no atmosphere, and therefore no clouds, clear observation was at all times possible—and every time the ghost star was studied even with the naked eye, it had become visibly larger. Until at last it became clear that it was time to be also watching Neptune for signs of the departing Neptunian people.

"Just one thing bothers me," the Amazon said.

"This ghost star will not produce any gravitational upheaval, since it's only an aggregation of light waves. If the Neptunians notice that before departure, they'll perhaps hesitate."

"I don't think so, Vi." Abna shook his bead. "It is a vital point upon which you've touched, I admit, and I confess I had overlooked it—but I think that the Neptunians will get away from their threatened world long before gravitational upheavals would have time to become appreciable. I sincerely hope so, anyway."

"And your hope is realized," Viona remarked, glancing up from the machine's telescopic equipment. "Unless the sunlight is playing me tricks, I believe I've picked up a fleet of space machines heading from Neptune in the direction of Uranus. Come and take a look."

CHAPTER NINE
SO FAR, SO GOOD

Abna moved quickly to her side and peered through the telescopic eyepiece. The immensely powerful lenses picked up a dozen glittering specks drifting away from Neptune in the direction of Uranus.

"Yes, they're on the move," Abna murmured in delight, moving aside for the Amazon to look. "Our decoy method seems to have worked perfectly. From now on we must keep ceaseless watch and see how many space machines leave that planet. We can then form a rough estimate as to whether any Neptunians have been left behind."

So a system of 'watches' was devised, one or the other of the trio always being at the telescope, and as hour succeeded hour, fleet after fleet sailed into the void from Neptune, until finally it seemed that the exodus was over and no more machines were visible. "It is to be hoped that everybody has gone," Abna said, when the Amazon, last on the watch, reported this fact. "It will make our task simpler. Even as it is, matters are simplified by the Neptunians leaving sooner than we expected. We shall not have to adopt extreme evading tactics on our trip."

"How soon are we going to make it?" Viona asked. "Sooner the better now, surely?"

"We go when the runaway is in a position to shield our approach," Abna replied. "Not before."

The Amazon said: "When we transport ourselves back to Earth, change places with our doubles, that is, we shall have to be sure if we can that our doubles are not with Quorne at the time; otherwise he will see the whole thing happen before his eyes."

"On Neptune," Abna replied, "they have the necessary telescopic-sound equipment to observe exactly what is happening to anybody on Earth. We shall have to transport it here, granting it has not been taken away. Altogether we shall need to bring back a considerable amount of equipment, so maybe we'd better use three of the six ships at our disposal, piloting one each."

"And when we get the equipment here—if ever we do—what do we use for power?" the Amazon inquired. "That is a point we do not seem to have thought of. Recording apparatus can be run from ordinary atomic batteries, I know, but equipment like the dissembler and telescopic-sound detector demands the maximum of power."

"Solar power is the answer," Abna replied. "The equipment you mention is normally run from solar generators. Two could give us all the power we need— so we'll get them."

"Even though they weigh around 500 tons each?" Viona questioned. "There are limits even to our strength, father."

Abna laughed. "True—but magnetic power, used by these space machines can do all the hard work and the void-cold won't hurt the equipment. Once in space it will just float along."

Abna waited until the gigantic ghost star seemed to be swallowing all heaven near Neptune—and also providing the perfect screen against those who might—indeed, would—be watching from Uranus.

"Another hour and we can start," he said.

All three knew exactly what they were going to do. Abna was to pilot the machine in which they had made their home, and the Amazon and Viona would take a machine each. So they donned space suits and presently set off to where the nearby machines stood. Entering them, they settled down at their respective control panels, waiting for Abna's departure signal.

"Ready!" came his voice through the loudspeakers, and immediately all three machines lifted swiftly from Pluto's inhospitable surface and sped into the void.

The Amazon found herself fascinated by the vision of that gigantic ghost star. Its light waves were so bright that they hurt the eye. Possibly the phenomenon was still millions of miles distant, but with the seconds it came nearer, forming a gigantic blazing curtain in front of the machines and effectively hiding them from watchers on Uranus.

"We need maximum velocity," came Abna's voice. "Use the automatic pilots and suspended animation. Every second of time counts from here on. Automatically we can cross the distance in forty-five minutes or less."

His instructions were obeyed. The Amazon put in the automatic pilot switches and then settled herself on the wall bunk, snapping on the button at her side which, from an overhead projector, produced radiation for creating suspended animation, automatically ceasing when 5.000 miles from Neptune's surface. Since Viona and Abna went through a similar voluntary relinquishment of consciousness, they knew no more until Neptune was looming before them, the ghost star close upon the planet and filling the void with its colossal area of blazing light photons.

Abna spoke over the radio: "All ready for the descent, you two? Let's go!"

Almost abreast the three machines plunged into the dense green of the Neptunian atmosphere and hurtled downward, using the detectors to guide them to that one segment where a duplicate region like that of Earth itself lay.

By the time they had located it, the ghost star had arrived, blanketing the planet in a shimmering, bewildering white translucence, as though the very air was burning with heatless fire. Exactly as Abna had anticipated, the mass of Neptune was holding the fake star for the time being—but it could not last indefinitely before forward momentum won the tug-of-war.

Then the second London came into view—dimly, because of the glittering haze. Quickly the Amazon switched on her x-ray detectors, but the screens showed no sign of life below, either in the buildings or below ground. It appeared that every Neptunian—including the Earthlings who had been transported to the planet—had departed to Uranus.

"Land in the main square," Abna ordered. "We must be as near to the controlling laboratories as possible—and, if those Neptunians took their equipment with them, all this has been in vain."

The ships landed close to the great building normally housing administration and scientific equipment. Quickly, the Amazon opened the airlock of heir machine and joined Abna and Viona outside. Around them the air was blurred with the configured light waves, but since they were as harmless as mist, the atmosphere itself was uncontaminated.

"Hurry!" Abna said curtly. "Every moment counts. The moment this star passes on, the Neptunians will realize that nothing here has been destroyed."

He was running as he spoke. Hurrying up the steps of the main building with the Amazon and Viona immediately behind him, he led the way to the master laboratory where the transition from Earth had been terminated. The lights came on as he opened the door, then he gave a sigh of relief.

A considerable amount of small equipment had been removed by the evacuating Neptunians, but the heavy stuff was untouched. Immediately Abna rushed to the repair section of the laboratory and brought out the necessary apparatus for unbolting the huge dissembly equipment from the floor. While he worked on this, the

Amazon and Viona carried projectors and recorders to their machines.

In ten minutes the smaller necessities had been moved. There remained the big material—the dissembler and its complementary switch panel, the reflector telescope, and the two enormous generators that operated from stored solar radiation.

"There's our problem," Viona said, surveying the heavy apparatus. "Can we take stuff of this size?"

"Yes," Abna replied. "Back to the ships and leave me to handle this."

All three of them immediately departed from the building, to discover that the mist of the ghost star was already commencing to thin as it moved on its way. Reaching their machines, the three closed their respective airlocks.

"You two start off," Abna ordered. "Set your course for Pluto so that Neptune is between you and Uranus, and remain on that course until you hear from me."

Abna watched them go and then closed the power switches of the atomic attractor bars fitted to the nose and stern of his vessel. On this occasion he used only the rear and gave it maximum current. Then he started the vessel upward.

It only crawled, exactly as he had expected it would, even though he was using enough recoil power to hurtle him into the void at high speed. The drag came from the equipment within the administration building. The attractor bars were struggling to pull to themselves everything of metal that was loose—and they did, with devastating effect.

Moving at a crawl of only 2,000 miles an hour, Abna drove his machine up, and down in the administration building chaos reigned. The huge dissembler and switchboard, together with the generators and telescope, smashed through walls and roofs in their efforts to reach the attraction dragging at them, and so immense was the power exerted they succeeded. Abna's eyes gleamed as, freed of the encumbrance of the shattered building around them, the generators and dissembler, together with the telescope and many other unwanted metal odds and ends, hurtled up into space and locked themselves to the attractor bars.

After a while, when Neptune's attraction was no longer a consideration, Abna cut off the attractors, with the result that the equipment floated freely in space, moving at exactly the same pace as the ship, chained by the simple law of mass.

"Good work," came the congratulating voice of the Amazon over the radio. "I didn't think there'd be enough power to do it."

"Neither did I. I think it was only using the maximum attraction and velocity that did it. Anyway, we have everything we need."

"And what are they going to think when they find the stuff gone?" the Amazon questioned grimly.

"I'm not particularly concerned. They can only guess, and if they transmit their opinion to Quorne, it will not signify because later on when the Neptunians are destroyed he'll still suspect us. But by then, we hope, our doubles will be in place. Don't worry over possibilities, Vi: we're doing all right so far."

In her own machine the Amazon shrugged to herself and said no more. She had not the philosophic temperament of Abna. She preferred to know—as nearly as possible—exactly how things would work out, and if she didn't, she was inclined to lose her grip. Since Abna seemed to have taken complete charge of the proceedings on this occasion, the problem was not hers.

CHAPTER TEN
BACK TO EARTH

The journey back to Pluto was made under normal conditions, without recourse to suspended animation, and Neptune was used constantly as a shield against watchers from Uranus—until at length the little world was so near that Abna gave the word to leave course and prepare for a landing. At this distance the space machines would never be sighted even with the most powerful equipment—and to judge from what they had left behind, the Neptunians had none with them.

Landing on Pluto again was complicated. A clear field had to be left for Abna first, so that he could juggle the attractors and lower the equipment safely. The Amazon and Viona had to keep their own space machines well in the clear, in case they too were snatched by the attractor bars. Even as it was, those vessels still left on the ground stirred uneasily as the intense magnetic currents passed around but never directly upon them.

Finally, however, Abna completed his task, and the dissembler and switchboard, the telescope in its mountings, and the massive generators lay safely at rest in the midst of the barren plain. Then it was possible to consider what move to make next.

"I have what I think is a good idea," Viona remarked, as they all three sat in one machine and partook of a meal of concentrates. "No one ship is big enough to house the equipment we've brought. Right?"

"Very right," Abna agreed.

"And we have to be enabled to work without space-suits, as though we're in a laboratory, so that our duplicates can return without finding themselves in an airless state which would instantly kill them?"

Abna and the Amazon both nodded and Viona's bright face broke into a triumphant smile. She spread her hands.

"Simple enough, then. We have six space machines here. Make five of them into one big one, like a mobile laboratory, and keep this one to live in—and to depart in if there should be a sudden emergency."

Abna did not make any quick reply, but at length he nodded.

"Yes—excellent," he agreed. "Fortunately we have tools and repair instruments on this machine—and on the others. We'll move five of the vessels so that they lie side by side and then cut out all except the end walls with flame welders. After that, we'll seal the joints and provide one large airlock at one end through which equipment can be levered."

In spacesuits, they worked to the limit of their stupendous physical strength. Magnetic attractors on the untouched space machine were used to drag the five other machines into position. After that the task was mostly internal, working with flame welders. At the end of six hours toil in their hot, cumbersome space-suits, the huge interior of the five interlocked machines had been created. The airlock itself came last, Abna fashioning it from the huge section of metal cut out to form the doorway. So at last the interior was sealed and the air pumps started to work. Since there were five, a steady current of air was assured.

This done, the three rested for awhile, then still impelled by the urgency of their task, they carried on again—but only after they had satisfied themselves through the ship's telescope that fleets of space machines were returning from Uranus to Neptune. The ghost star had receded to a hardly measurable speck on the face of infinity.

"Time grows short," Abna observed. "All the Neptunians will soon have returned. When they find their equipment gone, they may suspect Pluto here as the cause and come to look for us. We have some grace, but not much."

Donning their spacesuits they hurried outside and commenced the hard task of moving the generators and dissembler and sound telescope into the newly-made 'laboratory'. Once again the magnetic attractors came to their aid, and after four hours of grueling labor, they had finished the job and had the heavy equipment in position and bolted down where necessary.

"All we need now are tests," Abna said. "First the generators. Let us see if they operate at this distance from the sun. They should. Pluto is not vastly far from Neptune and they work perfectly there."

"I'll focus up the telescope and see what Earth has to tell us," the Amazon said.

"And I'll test out the dissembler," Viona said, moving towards it.

So each worked on his or her particular task—with good results. The generators operated at perhaps seventy-five per cent of their original power, but it was quite sufficient. The magnetic beams by which they drew their power from the far distant sun functioned as normally as could be expected at such a distance from the primary.

"Take a look," the Amazon said, and indicated the screen of the telescope.

Abna and Viona were silent, viewing Abna II. He was in a glass-walled space that overlooked a gigantic factory. In the factory itself was a hazy vision of half-completed space machines with Earth workers crawling around and over them.

"Good work," Abna said, glancing at the Amazon. "How did you manage to pick him up that easily?"

"On the indicator here the Neptunians have put the light-wave number of every Earth double, presumably for reference and quick study, and the number of our doubles are amongst them. Just set the pre-selector and there it is. In some ways the telescope is ahead of the one I invented for myself."

"What about the doubles of yourself and Viona?" Abna asked. "Find them as quickly as possible, Vi.

We've got to have some quick action before any Neptunians think of coming this way."

She nodded and operated the complicated controls, the powerful generators humming musically as they supplied the power for the amazing instrument. The scene on the screen blurred and slashed itself with electronic traceries—then a view of Amazon II appeared. She was by herself in an observatory, studying a series of cosmic charts, the view of a telescope behind her.

"My observatory," the Amazon exclaimed bitterly. "And wearing the black clothes I wear in space—and which I certainly could do with at this moment."

"She's alone, that's the point," Abna interrupted. "Now, Viona's double."

Viona II, in overalls, was in the midst of computing a sheet of figures. So distinct was the view, the heading of "Master Laboratory Report on Supplies" could be read clearly.

"And Quorne," Abna said, his voice urgent.

The Amazon looked for his light wave number and then made the adjustments again. Quorne appeared gradually. He was in a well-furnished room, eating a meal by himself and obviously lost in thought.

"Apparently he has made good use of our home," the Amazon said bitterly, switching off. "Well, what happens now?"

"First, clothes," Abna said. "We've no apparatus for making them here, so I'll have to resort to mind for that small effort. It shouldn't take long."

He became silent, his brow wrinkled with concentration, and after a while there appeared on the floor a black costume and gold belt for the Amazon, overalls for Viona, and a long smock—such as his double had been wearing—for himself.

"That settles that," he said. "We can be identically dressed, and we must hurry while Quorne is absent from our doubles. Now let us get our destruction thoughts recorded in readiness."

The amazing machines for recording thought waves were set up and for ten minutes the trio concentrated into them the most destructive mind-pictures they could conceive, the basic thought behind all of them being total destruction of living matter as opposed to total destruction of everything. The loss of Neptune itself in the devastating mental cataclysm would produce the most disturbing effects upon the Solar System as a whole.

"Vi, check up again on Quorne," Abna said, when the spell of concentration was over. "I have this recorder to switch back to the start, and hypnotic orders to prepare so that our doubles will obey when they return. Viona, you can start getting into the overalls."

Viona obeyed and the Amazon turned her attention to the telescope. Since the reading was still on Quorne, he automatically appeared on the screen after a brief interval. He had finished his solitary meal and was seated at the writing desk so familiar to the Amazon, busily computing. This scene she held until Abna had finished his concentration into the hypnotic projectors, and had determined that the mind records were so trained that the impact of their output would strike the rock-depression outside when needed.

"I think we are about ready now," he said. "I have recorded the necessary orders and worked out the relevant mathematics so that our doubles will not release the projectors until Pluto is exactly in line with Neptune, which will be fairly soon. Better get changed, Vi. We're ready to go."

The Amazon took the black costume and belt Abna handed to her and then hurried away to the sleeping quarters to change. Viona glanced at Quorne on the radio-screen and then back to her father.

"When our doubles have done the job required of them, what happens?" she asked. "To them, I mean."

"They die," Abna replied simply, and Viona looked surprised.

"Die! That is unlike you, father. I could understand mother taking such a step without a single qualm—but not you."

"They are enemies, and I am a realist in a battle of interplanetary dimensions," Abna replied. "If those doubles of ours were to remain alive after accomplishing their task, they could talk far too much should any Neptunians survive and come this way to investigate. They could also perhaps find means to communicate with Quorne, or he with them, and so upset our entire scheme. The only solution to that is death. I have arranged that when these projectors have concentrated three-quarters of their power at Neptune—sufficient to wipe out every inhabitant on that planet—they will swing round automatically and concentrate the remaining quarter of destructive thought-radiation directly upon our doubles. Though the waves will not be amplified by the rock area, they will nonetheless be devastating enough to wipe out that trio at such close quarters."

"Apparently," Viona commented, "nothing has been overlooked."

"Correct. Nothing has."

At that moment the Amazon returned in her familiar black outfit, buckling the golden belt about her waist. She fastened back her hair quickly and then glanced at the screen where Quorne still sat computing.

"I think we can risk it," Abna said, setting the triple directional-finders of the dissembler. "The dissembler will, of course, pick out our three doubles automatically wherever they may be."

"My double is obviously in my own observatory," the Amazon said. "And that's only a few yards away from the lounge where Quorne is now seated. Let's hope he remains there! Well, I'm ready if you are."

Abna gave a last look around him to make sure that nothing had been overlooked and that all the necessary devices would operate, or cut themselves off as needed—then he joined the Amazon and Viona on the big dissembly plate beneath the enormous electromagnets.

Reaching out he switched on the power and the surroundings blanked into darkness in the midst of intolerable anguish.

CHAPTER ELEVEN
"UP AGAINST A PROBLEM"

Shaken, breathing hard, the Amazon found herself lying on the floor beside the main bench in her own observatory. For a second or so she was almost incapable of thought as nerves and mind vibrations swung themselves back into their appointed paths; then she got slowly to her feet and gradually got the mastery of her reactions.

In front of her were a number of star charts of Andromeda, together with a mass of data, which evidently referred to charting a course through the void as far as the First Galaxy. She had gotten that far studying the charts intently when Quorne came in.

"Any sign yet of those frightened idiots returning to Neptune?" he asked briefly.

The Amazon glanced up and quickly simplified her thoughts as much as possible so that Quorne, if he decided to use his telepathic powers at all, would not be able to glean from her thoughts that she had replaced her double.

"I—I don't know," she replied, hesitating.

"Then it's time you did!" Quorne's boring purple

eyes impaled her, "I gave you orders to watch Neptune carefully once that star had gone on its way. Why don't you do your job properly?"

"I'm sorry. These charts were absorbing me."

Quorne made an irritated movement and strode to the telescopic reflector.

The Amazon had no idea how her double had behaved, and the slightest variance in characteristics might spell disaster. So she used her powers of telepathy whilst Quorne's attention was absorbed by the mirror. From his mind she gradually gathered a complete picture of the character her double possessed. It seemed as though Quorne sensed that his mentality was being invaded, for he abruptly turned and gave the Amazon a long look. She returned it unflinchingly, blanking her mind.

"How far have you proceeded with working out a course?" he asked finally.

"That is for you to say, Sefner Quorne. Since you have no faith in anybody but yourself it would he a waste of time my telling you how far I've progressed."

Quorne's eyes glinted. "I've told you before about your insolence, Amazon II. Do you require another sharp reminder that I am master here—?" He broke off as the radio buzzed. Immediately he hurried to it and switched on. "Sefner Quorne answering," he said. "Come in."

"Dral communicating," came the thin voice of the master of Neptune. "We have returned to our planet, as perhaps you are aware?"

"I was not aware," Quorne retorted acidly. "I leave a fool of a woman here in charge—Amazon II—and she fails to make observations. I observe, however, that you all scuttled like a lot of rats before a mirage. Your world was never in danger. That phenomenon was a ghost star."

"So we know—now; but there was nothing to distinguish it from the real thing—"

"It had no gravitational influence. That should have made the matter clear enough to you. You just couldn't wait to escape, could you? A ghost star is not so unusual an occurrence. They do appear from time to time, but they do not as a rule follow an orbit which carries them into our System."

"There are some things I do not understand, Quorne," Dral said. "We made some surprising discoveries upon our return here."

"Discoveries?" Quorne's voice sharpened. "In what way?"

The Amazon tensed and her gaze strayed from Quorne's urgently tensed back to the mercuroid mirror upon which Neptune was still clearly pictured.

"We discovered that some equip—"

Dral stopped dead. The Amazon looked up sharply. Quorne muttered something and adjusted the controls.

"Hello! Come in, Dral! Come in!"

The Amazon looked back at the mirror. For a moment she saw something stirring over its green surface. It was as impalpable as wind itself and yet it possessed irresistible power. Something unseen agitated the dense atmosphere to violent turbulence, but what happened below it was completely masked. As the silence from Neptune continued, she began to understand and breathed more freely.

"Dral, what's the matter?" Quorne demanded. "Has your equipment broken down? If you can hear me and I cannot hear you, make a light signal."

He gave up his attempts with the radio controls and rose quickly from his chair. Reaching the mirror, he gazed into it. By this time the mysterious swirling had almost ceased, and if he noticed this at all Quorne put it down to atmospheric variations.

The Amazon watched with him, but time passed and there came no sign of a signal. The radio, too, remained silent.

"Very strange," the Amazon remarked at length, and Quorne nodded slowly.

"Very. Dral has emergency equipment if the main radio apparatus fails: I can't understand why he does not use it."

"I would suggest you use the fine-focus on this telescope and see if you can penetrate to Neptune's surface," the Amazon suggested. "It might be possible to find out what has happened."

"Do it," Quorne ordered curtly.

Taking care not to appear too certain of her movements—for having made the telescope herself she knew all its manifold intricacies—the Amazon adjusted it, deliberately taking her time until Quorne became impatient with her slowness and elbowed her roughly out of the way. She nearly forgot herself and retaliated, then, just in time remembered. One display of her gigantic strength and the trick would fail.

Gradually Quorne adjusted the telescope to his liking and a near view of Neptune's surface—the area devoted to Earth duplication at least—came into view. Stupefied, he looked down upon a scene he could not understand. In all directions—in the streets and squares—lay bodies. They were completely motionless. As though stricken by a plague, not a solitary individual in the great duplicate-London city was moving.

"What in cosmos has happened to them?" Quorne whispered, without looking up. "Are they dead, unconscious, or what? What could cause this phenomenon?"

The Amazon inwardly congratulated herself upon the efficiency of Abna's thought-projection scheme that had produced this result, then she answered innocently: "My opinion is of little use, I assume, but I'd suggest that the ghost star left a mephitic gas behind which has overwhelmed every being on the planet."

"Possibly, but— No, I don't believe that!" Quorne shook his head vigorously. "When he returned to his city, Dral would immediately take air tests. That would only be logical. It is something much more significant than that." He looked again into the mirror. "Just as though they had all suffered some monstrous, concussive shock!"

The Amazon did not comment.

"It seems to me that the only way to solve the difficulty is to visit Neptune, and find out," he said at length. "For me to go personally with so many plans on the point of fruition would he impossible—but you could go. In fact, for all the use you are, you could take Abna and Viona with you."

The Amazon shrugged. "Very well. But it is hardly likely that our intelligence will be able to solve the problem. It will take a scientific specialist such as yourself."

"Nonsense!" Quorne waved a hand briefly. "With instruments you can find out as much as I could. You will go there, make a full reading on the apparatus of the atmosphere and radiation conditions, and then return here with the instruments sealed. I have got to know what has happened. Without your race in my plans, I have one of my main campaign props taken away from me."

"When would you wish us to go?" the Amazon asked at length.

"Within a few hours. We can't afford to let this business go unexplained. Have Abna and Viona come here, and I will explain to all three of you exactly what you must do."

With that Quorne left the laboratory, evidently to plan what he should do next. The Amazon hesitated, not at all sure where to locate Abna and Viona, so finally she issued a city-wide broadcast.

Quorne evidently did not hear it, for he did not come in to ask why she had used such a method. At least it proved successful, for Abna and Viona soon arrived, entering the residence by the rear door that took them through the observatory in order to get into the house.

"Vi!" Abna murmured, grasping her gently for a moment. "You materialized safely, then."

"Yes—and evidently you and Viona did, too. We are up against a problem, Abna. The Neptunians have been destroyed, presumably by our doubles—but Quorne has told me he's sending the three of us to investigate. That's the very thing we don't want. Only by staying here can we possibly overthrow the grip he's got on the people."

"I see." Abna thought for a moment. "The mind-wave idea worked as we planned it, then?"

"Perfectly. Take a look at that telescope mirror."

Abna and Viona did so, smiling grimly at the scene of the Neptunians lying dead from the onslaught.

"Good work," Abna commented. "And by this time our doubles ought to be dead, too."

"Quorne is waiting for us in the house to tell us what we must do."

She led the way from the laboratory and presently she, Abna and Viona presented themselves in the lounge where Quorne was sitting musing in a deep armchair.

He said: "I assume all three of you now know the circumstances concerning Neptune?"

"The Amazon gave us the details," Abna agreed.

"Very well. I have decided you three shall leave for Neptune and investigate. You will require several—"

"May I make a suggestion?" Abna put in quietly.

"That depends upon its nature. What is it?"

CHAPTER TWELVE
TRIVIAL ERRAND

"Apparently this mystery which has overwhelmed our race is no ordinary occurrence. It couldn't have been the ghost star which caused it, either, since that object could only have been made of light waves and as harmless as a mirage. The happening was on a huge scale, apparently, involving everybody on the planet. That points to enormous power somewhere. We know of only three people who might conjure up a power such as that—and three people with a reason for wishing our race out of the way. I mean the Golden Amazon, Abna, and Viona, of course."

The Amazon, gathering what Abna was driving at, took up the conversation.

"We do not know, Sefner Quorne, that those three are dead," she pointed out. The last we heard of them they had been wrecked on Pluto and scouts were sent to investigate— The scouts never reported, or if they did, we heard nothing about it."

"Yes—very true." Quorne agreed. "I just wonder, Abna II, if you are correct. I have little faith in your mental processes as a rule, but on this occasion—it is just possible. I have said repeatedly that as long as those three live—or at least are not known to be absolutely dead—they might be capable of anything. But what could they have done from a barren world like Pluto?"

"What can those three not do?" the Amazon asked. "I would remind you that Dral was about to say he had discovered something unusual upon returning home when he was cut off. If we could discover what he was going to tell us, the answer might be apparent."

"Yes, possibly." Quorne admitted, and he looked surprised. "You have more sagacity than I thought, Amazon II. Perhaps you'll be a useful aide even yet. Very well, you know what you have to look for on Neptune."

"Or Pluto," Abna said quietly. "Perhaps the source of our problem lies there."

"Investigate both planets," Quorne instructed.

"I would remark that if our originals are on Pluto," the Amazon put in, "we shall never return with any information. If they can destroy an entire race, as seems likely, we shall certainly present easy targets. We have had no experience of dealing with these super-scientists, and our own knowledge is infinitely below theirs."

"A fact of which I am bitterly aware," Quorne replied, and fell to thought. Presently he looked up. "Annoying though it is, it appears that I shall have to investigate this mystery myself," he said. "Not that the mystery so intrigues me—you three could deal with that with instruments. But the risk of my greatest enemies being still alive is one I can't afford to take. I am the only person with the ability to deal with them."

"Exactly so," Abna agreed calmly.

Quorne got to his feet. "Very well. While I am absent, all plans for the furtherance of our campaign must be held in abeyance. In you three I delegate my authority of control. You will make no new laws and revoke none of the existing ones. Keep the people working as they are until I return—and remember, I shall know exactly how you are behaving since the normal broadcasts will carry daily information to me out in space."

"Everything will be handled satisfactorily," the Amazon promised. "Rely on that."

"For your own sakes it had better be. Now pay attention while I show you what must be done during my absence. There are many tasks for these Earth fools to complete."

Six hours later Sefner Quorne departed into space, entirely unaware of how completely he had played into the hands of his enemies.

As the Amazon, Abna, and Viona stood in the laboratory observatory and watched the spaceship receding on the telescopic mirror, Viona said: "Eventually he'll come upon our three doubles—dead, we trust. What will happen then?"

"He'll think his three greatest enemies have been destroyed, so he'll endeavour to come back here and resume his activities," Abna said. "We'll allow him to come as near as we think comfortable, and then release upon him radiation that will shatter him utterly, mentally and physically. Quorne will be absolutely disintegrated, mind included."

The Amazon gave a sharp glance. "Mind included? How do you propose to do that?"

"I have yet to work it out, but I'll do it. You said yourself that Quorne's mentality must also be destroyed if we are ever to be free of him completely. And it will be. Mind force is only a vibration and capable of disintegration even as matter is. I'll work out the details later. Let us get other things straight first—informing the people that we are liberators, for instance, instead of imagined oppressors."

"Better be careful how we do it," Viona warned. "If one hint goes out over the radio bulletins, we'll have Quorne back here fast. And if no broadcasts go out at all, he'll be just as suspicious the other way. We also have to remember that there are hundreds of Neptunians on Earth here who have taken the place of original Earth people. They will be against us, and true to Quorne. Yet if we explain to the masses, we're bound also to explain to them."

Abna smiled indulgently and gave the Amazon a glance. "The child has definite wisdom," he commented. "She looks beyond the immediate present to a possible development—a trait she must have inherited from you Vi."

"Possibly." The Amazon dismissed the fact briefly. "Return to our problem. What do we do?"

Abna answered: "We know that every genuine Earth

person has a particular energy quotient, or as you call it, Vi, a personal aura. Your detector-compass is based on that principle, is it not? Very well. We learn the energy quotient of a bogus Earthling, note how much it varies from that of a genuine one, and then proceed to carefully single out every Neptunian. It will take time, no doubt, but not perhaps as long as we think, as the percentage of Neptunians to Earthlings is small. Once we have done that and determined where they are, we contrive to get every one of them in a particular spot and annihilate them."

"Entirely satisfactory!" the Amazon agreed, never averse to a plan of complete ruthlessness. "And to summon a Neptunian here will be simple, since he will believe he is serving his original masters—Neptunians, that is."

She picked up the desk visiphone and contacted the city controller. His face appeared on the screen—apparently quite an Earthly face, but Quorne had stated that the man was a Neptunian in Earth form, even though his appearance was identical to the man who had originally been the genuine controller of the city.

"You have received information that Sefner Quorne has departed to investigate our home planet," the Amazon said. "Kindly report here immediately for special orders."

"Very well." The controller's lack of respect was obvious, and it was occasioned by the fact that he believed the Amazon was only one of his own race, and not a very intelligent one at that, patterned after a superwoman.

"We will have the detector ready when he comes," the Amazon said, glancing at Abna. "I leave that to you."

He nodded and moved toward the instrument. Once he was satisfied that it was working correctly, he fixed up a remote control so that the controller would have no idea what was transpiring.

When the controller arrived, Viona admitted him and led him into the laboratory.

"Well?" he asked the Amazon curtly. "What do you want?"

The Amazon eyed him. "I think you would do better to moderate your tone, controller. Remember that while Sefner Quorne is away full authority is vested in us—equally."

"I'm aware of that, but you are still underlings to me and I never kowtow to underlings. Quorne has often spoken of your low level of intelligence, even if you have the physical vestment of super beings."

"Sit down," the Amazon said, motioning to a chair.

The controller obeyed, unaware that the chair had been placed so that his back was to the detector apparatus. Abna, apparently engaged in sorting check sheets, lowered his hand to the remote control switch buried amid a pile of correspondence on the drafting table, and in that second the energy quotient of the controller was duly registered.

"I sent for you," the Amazon explained, "to inform you that there is to be no radical change in the actual control of the city. Sefner Quorne was insistent upon that—but henceforth all orders which normally pass through you will pass through us instead, and we shall decide whether allocations of metals, chemicals, or whatever it may be shall be allowed or not."

"Very well." The controller's face was irritated. "And did you send for me just to tell me that?"

"Certainly. I did not do it over the visiphone, because they are not always as private as one would wish. We cannot afford to let anything leak out."

"I don't see that that instruction is in any way suspicious," the controller snapped, rising. "I have lost a lot of time on this trivial errand. However I suppose one cannot expect much else of underlings."

The Amazon's yellow hand tightened on the steel arm of her chair and it bent slightly. The controller looked vaguely surprised for a moment, then took his departure.

"That settles him, the Amazon commented, rising from her chair. "Did you get his reading Abna?"

"I surely hope so." He was busy examining the detector and presently he smiled. The recording needle pointed to 3,760.

CHAPTER THIRTEEN
QUICKLY DEALT WITH

"This should be easy," the Amazon remarked. "His reading—and therefore that of all Neptunians—is 1,500 above that of Earthlings' readings. All we have to do now is order all Neptunians on Earth to one particular place for a supposedly special reason, and then check up on the remaining inhabitants en masse. A projector trained on the populace, reactive to this particular energy quotient, will reveal instantly if any Neptunians have not obeyed our order. That way we can weed them out. The possibility is that they will all obey the orders given them and save us a lot of trouble."

"And until we've done that, we don't tell the people anything?" Viona asked.

"Most certainly not." The Amazon reflected for a moment and then gave Abna an inquiring glance. "Any suggestions as to what order we can give to force the Neptunians to gather in one spot?"

"We can say that Quorne left orders with us to have certain alterations made to Atlantic Island," he replied. "A task which Neptunians only can perform because their general intelligence is higher than that of average

Earth people. I think that would sound convincing enough. Naturally, once we have all of them gathered there, we'll destroy them."

The Amazon nodded, entirely satisfied with the suggestion. Atlantic Island was a synthetic creation of rock existing in the middle of the ocean, and used as a safe proving base for dangerous scientific experiments. Once gathered there, it would be simple to wipe out the Neptunians from the air without peril to normal people.

When the controller reached his office he sat thinking. His expression was perplexed. Finally he pressed the button, which signalled one of his Neptunian colleagues—the minister responsible for public affairs, and, like the controller, a duplicate of the original.

When he arrived, the controller motioned to a chair.

"Have a seat, Hilton," he invited. "I want your opinion. I've discovered something so disturbing I don't trust myself to take action. You know all the details concerning our home planet—how it was threatened by a ghost star which afterwards passed on into the infinite?"

"I know all the details," Hilton answered grimly. "Including the news about the rest of our race being mysteriously obliterated."

"Then you will also be aware that Quorne has gone to investigate, leaving behind him the duplicates of our three enemies—the Amazon, Abna, and Viona. A little while ago I was summoned by the Amazon to receive some orders, trifling in the extreme and certainly hardly worth the time it took—but just as I was leaving I noticed a strange thing. The Amazon resented a remark I made about her and in anger she gripped the arm of her chair—a steel tube bar. It bent visibly under her grip. Only a hand of colossal strength could produce an effect like that."

"Are you suggesting," Hilton asked, "that you somehow saw the real Amazon?"

"That is what I believe—yet I can't imagine how it could be so. The Amazon's double would never have the strength to bend a steel bar."

Hilton's face began to look gray with uneasiness. "If you are right, controller, we are in a desperate position. If that woman is the Amazon, then Abna and Viona may also be real and not the doubles. But how could such a thing happen without Quorne knowing? It isn't possible."

"To those three scientists I think anything is possible," the controller answered. "I wanted your reactions—and your support—since I intend to radio Sefner Quorne in space immediately. He must return and investigate. Come with me."

Hilton rose from his chair and followed the controller to the immense radio-television transmission rooms in the building.

"Leave us," the controller ordered briefly, and the chief operator vacated his post, leaving the main transmission studio empty.

Seating himself, Hilton standing behind him, the

controller set to work with the instruments, using the special waveband that penetrated into the depths of space.

"Controller calling Sefner Quorne," he said, when the detector showed he had reached a fast-moving body in the void. "Come in, please."

"Sure this is safe?" Hilton asked anxiously. "If this communication should be picked up by the Amazon—if it is she—what will happen to us?"

"A most unlikely happening," the controller answered. "This is a sealed wavelength and nobody else can contact it."

But the Amazon had gone to her own radio for the transmission of her message to the Neptunians, to instruct them all to gather on Atlantic Island. The moment she switched on her apparatus she noted the interference-needle, which was jammed against the maximum reading. Such was the delicacy of her equipment, it recorded in a moment if the airwaves were not clear.

"Somebody is certainly monopolizing the air," she commented, motioning Abna and Viona to her. "Look at that."

"Whoever it is, they're using radio illegally," Viona remarked. "No broadcasting is permitted without reference to us first. Quorne said as much."

"I'm aware of it." The Amazon adjusted the radar-detectors until the outflowing currents struck the edge of the unknown carrier-beam reaching out into space. On a screen appeared the familiar tracery of lightning flashes.

"Very powerful and very extensive," Abna murmured. "Reaching out directly into space, apparently."

"I can think of only one person in space to whom anybody might wish to communicate, and that's Quorne," the Amazon commented. "Ah! Here's the wavelength!" she added, as the beam-analyzer needle swung delicately and finally came to rest. She adjusted the tuner on the panel and after a moment or two, the 'pirate' broadcast came in clearly.

"...and I can only hope that you are receiving me, Sefner Quorne. No answering signal from you makes me wonder. As I have said, I cannot imagine the double of the Golden Amazon having the strength to bend a steel bar. Which means the Amazon is here—and possibly Abna and Viona as well. I am convinced that you should return immediately and investigate this matter."

The Amazon glanced up sharply into the faces of Abna and Viona. They were looking at her in surprise.

"What's he talking about?" Abna asked. "When did you ever forget yourself so far as to bend a steel bar?"

"He said something I didn't like when he came here," the Amazon replied. "It is the controller speaking. His voice is unmistakable. I gripped my chair arm and it bent. I didn't think he noticed."

"Evidently he did and this is serious," Abna snapped. "Of all the idiotic things to do! Why didn't you control yourself?"

"I forgot." The Amazon's face was bitter. "So might anybody. Apparently we are safe so far, since Quorne hasn't replied. The possibility is he is not receiving the message—"

"Come in, Sefner Quorne," the controller's voice broke in urgently. "Controller calling Quorne! Are you receiving me? Minister Hilton is ready and waiting to verify my statement."

"Oh, is he?" the Amazon muttered. "That makes two of them—and apparently Quorne still isn't answering. Abna, take over. I'm going to deal with those two before this goes any further."

Abna nodded, and before he could ask any questions the Amazon had left the laboratory swiftly. In a matter of moments she had her powerful atomicar out of the garage and was soon driving at top speed along the main road to London. It seemed a logical assumption to her that the 'pirate' broadcast must be coming from the administration building in the heart of the city, and to that building she drove. The sentries saluted as she entered, wondering vaguely at the determined look on her yellow face and the lithe speed of her movements.

Reaching the radio department, she glanced about her sharply and then summoned one of the technicians. He came hurrying over promptly.

"Where is the controller?" she snapped.

"I last saw him entering the main transmission studio, Amazon, with Minister Hilton."

"Thank you." The Amazon hurried on, gained the studio, and opened the door swiftly. Once on the other side of it, she closed and locked it, her violet eyes fixed on the two men at the apparatus.

"Calling Sefner—" the controller began wearily, and then the Amazon's voice, knifed across his own.

"Stop that communication!"

Both men swung round as the Amazon approached them.

"You are observant, controller," she remarked. "My mistake in not controlling my strength led you to deduce quite a lot. I am the original Amazon, and I do not approve of the communication you sent to Sefner Quorne."

"But how could you know what I—"

The controller stopped, baffled. Then with a sudden gasp of alarm Hilton made a wild dash for the door. Knuckles of steel smashed into his face and he recoiled backwards, toppling to the floor.

"You are as much in this as the controller, my friend," the Amazon said. "Whether or not Quorne has received your message is not clear, since he doesn't seem to have answered—but I certainly do not intend to allow either of you to have a second chance!"

For a split second the controller hesitated, then his hand flashed down to his pocket, presumably to withdraw a weapon. But he stood no chance against the Amazon's greater speed. In one movement her atom gun leaped from her belt into her fingers and she fired.

The controller dropped, a burn-hole driven straight through him.

Hilton scrambled up from the floor to find the

Amazon's violet eyes fixed upon him.

"Amazon, I had nothing to do with this!" he insisted. "I was sent for by the controller and—"

"Your misfortune lies in knowing as much as you do," the Amazon broke in. "And you are no more to be trusted with the fact that I am the Amazon than is any other member of your race. I've only one way to silence you."

"But, Amazon, I tell you—" Hilton stopped, his fascinated eyes watching the pencil of fire leaping at him.

The Amazon put her gun away as she surveyed the sprawled bodies, then she stepped to the radio equipment and quickly altered the dials so that the special space wavelength was completely lost. Then she unlocked the door and went into the radio room, summoning to her the nearest technician.

"There seems to have been some kind of trouble between the controller and Minister Hilton," she said. "You will find their bodies in there. Remove them. I will consult Sefner Quorne in space as to who shall take their places."

The technician looked blank but did not question the order, and the Amazon went on her way, returning home within a few minutes. As Abna and Viona looked at her inquiringly, she explained what she had done.

"And do you suppose, when the news gets out, that it will be believed that those two killed each other?" Viona asked.

"I don't know—and I don't care. The only way to

silence those two was to kill them. Our one hope is that Quorne did not receive the message. I suppose he made no reply during the time I was away?"

"None," Abna answered. "Best thing we can do is get all the Neptunians to Atlantic Island as arranged, and then deal with them quickly. If Quorne did get that message and returns, we must be ready for him—an for any Neptunians whom we don't manage to eliminate. You drafted out the order, Vi: better get it broadcast."

CHAPTER FOURTEEN
PREPARING FOR REVENGE

There was a very good reason for Quorne not having received the message sent to him. So great was his speed in the plunge across space to Neptune he had placed himself in voluntary suspended animation, leaving the automatic controls to guide the vessel and awaken him when he was near Neptune. So, when he was within a million miles of the green-tinted world, he began to revive and slowly knitted together his stupefied wits.

He surveyed outside, refreshed himself with a meal, and then turned to the instruments. The radio apparatus was demanding attention by reason of its recording light glowing. Whatever messages had been sent during his spell of enforced sleep had been recorded in full and automatically switched back to start so that he could now hear them.

In astonished and then venomous mood he listened to the report the controller had sent him, finishing with its almost desperate request to know whether the message had been received. His eyes glinting with anger, Quorne stood up and looked outside. He was almost upon Neptune and forced to make a quick decision. Either he could descend to the planet and try to discover what had wiped out the Neptunian race, or he could return to Earth and deal with his three enemies who had apparently completely duped him.

"Unless the man's raving," he mused, "I cannot see how even the Amazon could perform a feat like that, replacing her double. And if it should be so, then I'll stand no chance if I try to return. On the other hand, there is this problem of Neptune to be solved, and maybe I can verify for myself if the genuine three really did find a way back to Earth, which I greatly doubt."

By the time he had come to the end of these speculations, the machine was fast approaching the Neptunian atmosphere. He settled quickly at the controls and guided the vessel to the area where Earth duplication lay. He landed in the main square of duplicate London, and tested the atmosphere before venturing outside. It gave a normal reading.

He collected a series of instruments, unfastened the airlock, then stepped to the exterior. The scene was exactly as he had seen it from Earth, and quite unchanged. As far as he could tell, not a single body had moved in the interval. His investigation was long and thorough and puzzled him all the more. There was no doubt that the bodies he had examined had all been blasted by some inconceivably powerful mental force, which had stunned the Neptunians into death by sheer shock.

Pondering, Quorne walked into the various buildings of the city, making notes as he went, and at length he came to the headquarters building to find Dral still at the radio equipment, slumped forward in death, with his assistants prone on the floor. Recalling the suddenness with which Dral's communication had ended, Quorne realized that death must have been instantaneous.

And presently his eyes strayed to other parts of the laboratory. In puzzled interest he noted the absence of the huge dissembler, two generators, recording equipment, and a high-powered telescope.

"Dissembler," he whispered, clenching his fists. "Gone! By the dissembler those three could have returned to Earth. But where is it?"

The answer he gave himself was the outcome of logic. It must be on Pluto, where he knew the three to have been stranded. For it to be anywhere else on Neptune was unlikely since, in that case, there would have been no need to remove it from the spot it had formerly occupied.

Quorne returned to his ship and headed for Pluto at the fastest possible speed, settling down finally at the 'five-ship laboratory', Protected by his spacesuit, he started a second investigation and ere long came upon the three bodies in the 'laboratory'—the Amazon, Abna, and Viona, or so they seemed to be. The sight of the dissembler half told him the truth and instruments told him the remainder. An examination of the three bodies satisfied him that they were the doubles and not the originals.

"Clever," he whispered to himself. "I am compelled to admit that fact. Ingenuity carried to its limit, as one can always expect with those three—but I wonder if they are so clever as they think? They must have used a mighty weapon to destroy the Neptunians. If I can find what it was, maybe I can use it, too, to destroy Earthlings in retaliation. Return I cannot, so destruction of that which I might have ruled is the only alternative."

He began a study of all the instruments and it did not take him long to reason out the details, particularly when at last his gaze was attracted by the peculiar copper glint of the rock depression not far from the 'laboratory'. He went to examine it—and since his thoughts were never particularly sociable, he received a terrific recoil kick from the rock depression when he unintentionally directed his thoughts towards it.

That was quite enough for Sefner Quorne. He was scientist enough to put the rest of the details together. The rock depression, the hypnosis projectors, the dissembler, the ultra-powerful telescope—they all fitted into place as pieces in the jigsaw.

He investigated until he found the air apparatus, switched it on, then when the air pressure was at normal, he removed his clumsy suit and set himself to ponder. His first move was to get the telescope into working order and train it on Earth. At last he was successful in pinpointing the Amazon, Abna, and Viona—all three of them together, as it happened, in the laboratory. The fourth-dimensional sound equipment began to carry their voices.

"According to that," Abna was saying, "everything is ready?"

"Everything," the Amazon responded. "The detectors have been trained over everybody comprising the populace, taking them in at several thousands a time, but there have been no adverse reactions on the needle, so evidently no Neptunians remain among them. We've herded them all to Atlantic Island and the rest should be simple."

The Amazon and Viona bent their heads over a sketch map and said nothing further, and Quorne switched off irritably, puzzled. Why all Neptunians should have been 'herded' to Atlantic Island he could not quite understand—and for that matter, did not particularly care. He had lost control of Earth: that was certain. So he must destroy.

"Whether I can or not depends on whether that thought-reflective area can hurl a thought wave, or series of waves, as far as Earth," he thought. "I cannot think why it shouldn't, because thoughts are the only known quantity in the Universe which do not decrease in power with distance."

He ceased musing to himself and plunged into the task of mathematics, basing his principle upon the recoil power he had received from the rock depression over a given distance. By the time he had come to the end of his calculations, he was satisfied that thought waves deflected to Earth would reach there with sufficient strength to wipe out every living thing—most certainly Earth people, possessing far less mental resistance than the Neptunians. If the Amazon, Abna, and Viona proved strong enough to overcome the onslaught, then he would have to deal with them separately afterwards. At least he would achieve his object and destroy those whom he could not now dominate.

This factor decided, he moved on to the next one—working out the relative positions of Earth and Pluto so that they would be in a straight line for a brief time as far as the rock depression was concerned.

Meanwhile, the Amazon, Abna, and Viona were aboard the gigantic *Ultra*, the one machine in which they had absolute faith when an important mission had to be accomplished. The vessel had six hydrogen bombs and three universal bombs—infinitely more devastating even than the H-bomb—in its rack, more than sufficient to blow Atlantic Island clean out of the ocean and reduce all those upon it to atomic dust.

"Seems a pretty merciless course," Abna mused, as the shores of England were left behind, "but I suppose it's the only one."

"Certainly it is." There was no hesitation in the Amazon's voice. "Every one or those Neptunians is a spy, and because of them, hundreds of Earth people on Neptune had to die when those thought waves were released upon that planet. It is only just that the counterparts should die also."

Abna did not say anything. Although he had complete disregard for matter structure, as such, there was the human element in him, which always recoiled a little before the coldly scientific conception of elimination that was the Amazon's main characteristic. As for Viona, she refrained from comment, knowing she would not be listened to in any case.

"I suppose," Abna resumed, as the Ultra fled on across the ocean, "we can count ourselves lucky that Quorne has not returned. I've been expecting him any moment."

The Amazon studied the course ahead and then said: "Then I think you'll be disappointed, Abna—or relieved, as the case may be. I don't think Quorne will ever return in person, because if he does know the facts he'll realize the united front that is against him. If he tries at all, as I very much believe he will do, it will be something whereby we cannot immediately retaliate— However, forget that for the time being. We are near our target."

A gleam came into the Amazon's violet eyes as synthetic Atlantic Island came into view far below. Upon it were the various low-built buildings that had formerly housed test scientists and now were occupied by the Neptunians awaiting the special orders of Quorne, which the Amazon had promised would follow.

"Stand by the bomb switch," the Amazon instructed. "You take the H-bombs, Abna—and you, Viona, the U-bombs."

They obeyed, standing ready by the switchboard. Down below, as the huge vessel cruised overhead, Neptunians—exactly like Earthlings—came into view.

"Now!" the Amazon ordered, and instantly Abna and Viona pressed the switches to which they had been assigned. The moment they had done so the Amazon threw the power switches to maximum and sent the *Ultra* screaming upward. Fast though the vessel moved, however, and crushing though the acceleration was, the colossal shock of the destruction of Atlantic Island sent concussion waves battering upward.

The *Ultra* lurched and twisted in the crazy air currents, recoiled under the battering of air blasts, and then very gradually the Amazon brought it under control again and began to descend once more toward the mighty mushroom of smoke hanging over the water where Atlantic Island had been. No trace of it remained—only the still agitated waters. No sign of a body, a trace of buildings—not a fragment of wreckage even.

"Entirely satisfactory," the Amazon commented. "I fancy we shan't have any more trouble from that direction."

CHAPTER FIFTEEN
A MISCALCULATION

She turned the *Ultra* and began to head back toward Britain. The Amazon was just on the point of saying something to Abna when she was seized by the most extraordinary sensation. In many ways it resembled that tearing anguish which was the inevitable accompaniment of transition by the dissembler, but in this case the reaction was more mental than physical. Something was tearing at her consciousness with such diabolical force that she could not speak for the moment. Into her brain flashed a series of fantastically horrible conceptions, each one aflame with death.

Apparently Abna and Viona were experiencing the same sensation, for they were striving desperately to remain standing, their hands to their foreheads. They, too, were bereft of the power of speech and required every scrap of their resistive will power to remain conscious. Only Abna succeeded. Viona turned pale, moaned, and then dropped heavily on the floor. The Amazon stared at her through blurred eyes and tried frantically to bring her thoughts into focus—without avail. The *Ultra*, bereft of her guiding hands, plunged crazily and entered into a power dive, screaming down toward the ocean. Not that the Amazon was aware of this for she, too, had become unconscious.

Abna made a colossal effort and reached the control panel just as the *Ultra* struck the water. The impact knocked him flying backwards and he collided with the wall. In that second the dreadful thrall that had held his mind relaxed and the space machine, tremendously tough in its construction, surged up to the surface of the waves and floated there unharmed. Abna shook himself, dizziness slowly retreating. He looked down at his broken arm and shoulder where he had hit the wall and in a matter of seconds mentally repaired the smashed bones and torn muscles.

Lifting Viona, he placed her on the wall bed and a few moments of mental rejuvenation on his part set the girl stirring again into life. By this time the Amazon was recovering of her own accord and she looked about her dazedly.

"What in creation hit us?" she asked at last. "Some kind of unexpected reaction from those bombs, do you think?"

Abna shook his head. "No, Vi, it was something much more potent and baleful than that. Those bombs couldn't produce a mental reaction; it would have been physical, if anything. I have the extremely uneasy feeling that when we come to investigate, we may find ourselves the last people in the world!"

"What!" The Amazon stared at him blankly.

He said: "There was mental force of inconceivable

violence in that onslaught."

"Quorne!" the Amazon cried, leaping up. "It must have been Quorne!"

"That's what I think," Viona said, rising rather unsteadily from the wall bed. "He did to us what we did to Neptune, which means he must have found that thought-reflective rock area on Pluto. Probably he'd have kept it up a great deal longer only the positions of the two planets were possibly not favourable."

The Amazon's yellow face had become mask-like in its vindictive hatred. "We'll see what damage he's done," she said, "and then settle with him."

"Settle with him?" Abna repeated. "How?"

"Go after him, of course! He probably thinks he's destroyed us, and that everything from now on is plain sailing—but he's extremely mistaken."

Her lips tight, the Amazon flung herself onto the control chair and in a few seconds had the *Ultra* climbing rapidly once more. It was only a matter of minutes before London was reached—but it was far from a city of the dead. There was a certain air of confusion apparent, particularly in the form of traffic darting back and forth from the huge medical centres, and in some streets, bodies were lying awaiting discovery.

"Apparently the attempt was incomplete," the Amazon said, a light of relief coming back into her eyes.

She swung the *Ultra* again, lowering it as her own home was reached. In the laboratory she switched on the radio and asked for details. In half an hour she knew the whole story. About three-quarters of the Earth's population had survived death, but many were deranged.

"For which there can only be one explanation," the Amazon said. "Quorne must have slightly miscalculated over such a tremendous distance and the effect was not complete. Also, he evidently didn't have time enough at his disposal, before Pluto swung out of alignment with Earth. The damage is considerable, as far as humanity is concerned, but it can be repaired. As for ourselves, we will go and look for Quorne and if possible deal with him, the moment I have broadcast the facts to the people."

She turned to the radio equipment, switched it on, and in a moment or two was delivering a worldwide broadcast. In it, she explained every fact, bringing the people up-to-date with events, and making clear to them the reason for the mental devastation that had so recently struck them. Though the resurgence of hope that went through the survivors was not apparent to the Amazon, Abna, or Viona, it was nonetheless there. The knowledge that the three greatest scientists had not really deserted them after all took an enormous weight from the shoulders of the people.

"And now for Quorne." The Amazon switched off the apparatus. "Our whole object from here on is to find him and bring to an end forever his constant depredations and insane ambition."

"And while we are gone?" Viona asked. "Do we leave Earth people to govern themselves?"

"They can do it. I have already explained to them, as you heard, that we might be absent an indefinite time while Quorne is dealt with. They will appoint their own leaders and sort themselves out while we are absent."

Abna said: "Let us be thoroughly sure of what we are doing and where we are going. Quorne may be expecting us. He must know that our minds might have proved too strong to be overwhelmed by the brief mental onslaught he directed this way."

"We go to Pluto," the Amazon said. Then surprisingly altered her resolve. "No. Better to search space first."

On a sheet of paper she wrote a few words, which were immediately self-explanatory.

"I have just remembered that if Quorne is on Pluto he will have the telescope trained on us, and will be able to hear what we are saying. We will go to Pluto as arranged, but let him think otherwise. This writing will be too small for him to read. Understand?"

"Right, we go into space," Abna agreed, as the Amazon bunched the note in her palm and threw it away. "And the sooner the better."

They did not exchange any further information until they were within the *Ultra*. Here they knew they were safe from all probing forms of radiation. Nothing could penetrate the vessel's triply-insulated walls, unless, perhaps, it was thought waves.

"Suppose," Abna asked, as the Amazon checked over the controls before departure, "Quorne makes another attempt to wipe out the remainder of Earth people? He'll know that he failed to do it properly, so there's nothing to stop him trying again whilst we're on our way to deal with him."

The Amazon reflected and presently gave a nod. "Yes. That's true enough. Lead and zilanite ores combined form an absolute insulation against the very short wavelengths of thought. I had better advise the people to construct helmets of those materials and wear them night and day until they are advised that all danger is past.... And during our journey we might do worse than manufacture an interior insulation for this machine of the same material."

Switching on the radio she gave a broadcast that she knew would at least be picked up by the city's receivers, and where her message did not reach it would be transmitted orally by those who did hear.

"The Golden Amazon speaking," she said. "It is possible that Sefner Quorne may make a second mental onslaught upon you—though that cannot come immediately because Pluto will not be in a favourable position regarding Earth. In the meantime, turn all your endeavours to the manufacture of helmets made of a quarter-inch thickness of lead and zilanite. Every man, woman, and child must wear one. In no other way can you be sure of immunity from mental attack. Those of you who hear this message, pass it on immediately, please. That is all."

The Amazon switched off and to Abna and Viona added, "If Quorne heard that it doesn't signify. Maybe it will make him realize that a second attempt will be useless.... Now, let us be on our way."

Below, there was a brief glimpse of people waving as the vessel swept over London—then it climbed steadily until it had plunged through the stratosphere and into the depths of space. The Amazon increased the acceleration until inertia-drag was equivalent to Earth-normal gravitation and then she got up from the control panel.

"We have a job to do," she reminded Abna and Viona. "We must prepare some inner lining for these walls."

They nodded and accompanied her into the fully equipped laboratory of machine tools and atomic blast furnaces with which the *Ultra* was equipped. For nearly six hours, while the *Ultra* swept onwards out beyond the orbits of the Moon and Mars, they were at work moulding them into place against the *Ultra*'s control room walls. Other parts of the vessel they left untouched, since they would be unlikely to be anywhere else but the control room when they neared Pluto—and Quorne.

"That should take care of the situation," the Amazon said, as they settled down to a meal in the control room. "No matter how much destructive thought vibration Quorne flings at us, it cannot have any effect."

"How about invisibility?" Viona suggested. "We can make the vessel invisible easily enough. In that way, if Quorne is still on Pluto, we can approach without him seeing us."

"Waste of power," the Amazon answered—and she

nodded to the fuel gauge. "We'll need all we can get if we have to pursue our friend across the Universe. In any case, all modern vessels, such as the one in which he left Earth for Pluto, are equipped with mass-detectors, and they'd show our presence even if we couldn't be seen optically. No, we'll advance openly and from such a direction that he will not be able to use the rock depression in a straight line upon us."

So it was decided, and a system of watches was arranged.

Then the Amazon increased the *Ultra*'s speed to half maximum, sending it winging across the void with stupendous velocity. Onward, hour after hour, devouring millions of miles of empty space, out beyond the orbit of vast Jupiter and magnificent Saturn. Then past Uranus, past Neptune, and so at last Pluto came into view, on the rim of the Solar System.

When this moment happened, the trio was in the control room, the 'watches' at an end. Behind were countless millions of miles of space and many weeks of Earth-time, though judging from the everopen radio—which had remained silent through the period—nothing untoward had happened.

"We'll approach from such an angle that it will bring us in behind the rock depression," the Amazon said, and settled at the controls.

CHAPTER SIXTEEN
VISITORS FROM ANOTHER WORLD

Presently they saw that the 'five-machine labora-tory' was still there, together with two other vessels.

"From the look of things, he's there," Abna said. "One of those machines is the one we left behind: the other must be his. What do you propose doing? Dropping bombs on the laboratory?"

"For Quorne something more effective is called for." The Amazon guided the *Ultra* swiftly downward as she spoke. "He must be destroyed mentally as well."

"Get him within range of that rock depression and have all three of us concentrate into it, and every mental and physical atom of his make-up will be destroyed," Viona said. "So it seems to me, anyhow."

"She is probably right," Abna agreed. "We should—"

He broke off and staggered sharply as the *Ultra* suddenly lurched as though from an upflung blast of an explosion. The Amazon looked outside in surprise, but nothing unusual was visible. Then it came again, this time with much more effect. The *Ultra* was dragged to a standstill in its swift downward flight, spun around dizzily, and then sent moving on a course over which the Amazon had no control whatever.

"Magnetic waves!" she exclaimed. "Quorne's using them somehow—"

The *Ultra* was forced to the rocky ground within about a quarter of a mile of the thought-reflecting rock area, and all the Amazon's efforts to force the power plant to move the machine were unavailing. In a fury she snapped on the radio.

"You there, Quorne?" she barked.

"That seems obvious," came his voice. "I have you firmly anchored, my friends, and you cannot get away."

"Don't be too sure!" the Amazon retorted.

"But I am! I gathered enough over the radio-telescope to realize you intended flying into space, though whether to Pluto or not was unclear. In any event, I decided that in the interval I would prepare a welcome for you. So I promptly flew to Neptune, brought away the most powerful magnetic attractors I could find, and set them up in readiness for your coming. You should have struck at me from about two miles' height, then I couldn't have saved myself."

"I have no wish to just destroy your body, Quorne," the Amazon told him. "I intend to wipe out your mind as well."

"From which I assume you believe you can wipe me out? A very unlikely prospect this time, Amazon. I observe that I cannot penetrate the walls of your machine and see within, so presumably you are heavily insulated—but thanks for leaving your radio aerial untouched which enables us to have this refreshing conversation. And it really is that, you know. I rarely have the chance of speaking to my equals in intelligence."

"Never mind the conversation, Quorne! We didn't fly all the way from Earth just for that!"

"Then what did you come for? Oh, yes, to destroy me! Well, how do you propose starting?"

The Amazon gave Abna and Viona a grim look while she searched in her mind for an answer: then Quorne spoke again.

"Since Abna and Viona boarded the *Ultra* with you upon leaving Earth, I assume they are still with you— which makes my picture complete. I have surrounded this spaceship laboratory with a field of force so that anything you may hurl at me will be instantly deflected."

"In that case it is a stalemate," the Amazon said, "for the *Ultra* is also completely protected. There is nothing you can do to destroy us even though you have the vessel magnetized."

"On the contrary there *is* something I can do to destroy you, which is why I have manoeuvred your vessel into that precise position. You are directly in line with that peculiar thought-reflecting area—"

"You still can't do anything," the Amazon interrupted. "This machine is insulated against thought-waves."

"A possibility that occurred to me, so I shall not waste time trying to penetrate. But do you believe your vessel—or you yourselves—can withstand the relentless crushing power of a small asteroid building up around you?"

The Amazon did not answer. She gave Abna and Viona a horrified glance and it was plain from their expressions that they, too, were taken aback by Quorne's diabolical conception.

"I have no proof of it," Quorne continued, "but I believe that the ghost-star which caused the great exodus from Neptune was entirely your own creation. You will realize therefore how simple is, with the aid of the reflective rock, to build up any desired form of matter from space itself. That is what I intend to do—create an asteroid with you in its core. You will be sealed within thousands of tons of constantly compressed rock, forming the centre of the asteroid itself. The larger it becomes, the more matter it accumulates, the greater will become the central pressure. And from it you will have no means of escape."

The Amazon reacted. She shot to her feet and dived for the airlock, intent on selling her life as dearly as possible as long as she escaped the threatened vessel. But she was too late. As she reached the outer airlock, ready in her spacesuit, a wall of dense matter formed outside, completely blocking her. She blasted her ray gun at it, but it had already become so thick that the beam failed to penetrate to its outer limit,

Her face grim, she returned the gun to her belt, closed the airlock, and then went back into the control room. The opaque windows showed that the gray matter of the thought-created asteroid was in every direction, solid rock formation.

"Well, what is the answer to this one?"

The Amazon had removed her spacesuit when she asked the question and Abna and Viona turned from the ports, where they had been studying the immovable prison that was binding them in.

Abna said: "This asteroid could not have been brought into being without Quorne's willpower being vastly amplified by that rock area. To aid our will power, we have the amplifiers that we use when hypnosis is necessary. Maybe we can defeat him mentally if not physically."

"We'll want these walls stripped of the inner insulation," Viona exclaimed. "Otherwise thought waves will not pass through them."

Abna assisted her with instruments to remove the plates whilst the Amazon set up three thought-amplifying hypnotic machines. Even as she worked, the *Ultra* creaked a little now and again as the accumulating weight of mind-created rock began to have an effect.

The Amazon, Abna, and Viona took up positions in front of the amplifiers—all of which were trained directly towards the position where they had last seen the 'spaceship laboratory'—and switched on the power. Then they concentrated with every vestige of their mental strength.

The conflict between Quorne's amplified thought waves and those battering back at him was tremendous, and owing to the enormous amplifying advantage he had, Quorne beat back the trio time and again, even Abna, who could usually manage to subject matter to his wishes.

From outside the *Ultra* there came a sudden cracking as one of the outer plates crumpled under the weight of rock building around it. Then there was silence.

Presently the Amazon said: "Has the asteroid ceased gathering rock? I don't hear any creakings or sounds of straining."

"Possibly," Viona said, "Quorne thinks he has made the asteroid big enough to crush us and isn't trying any more. He has no means of knowing whether we are crushed or not, if it comes to that."

"Yes, that's probably it," the Amazon agreed, her face brightening. "We'll wait for a while: then if nothing happens, we'll see if we can manage to move some of the rock by mind force."

But the reason for Quorne's cessation of activities was vastly different from that which the trio imagined. In fact, Quorne could hardly believe the manifestation and stood spellbound at the nearest window of the 'spaceship laboratory'.

Not very far away a vessel like that of a space machine, but with many novel features upon it, was appearing. Where it had come from, Quorne had not the slightest idea, for he had only just noticed it. It lay to one side of the straight line to the rock amplifying area and therefore had escaped the mental waves. It seemed to Quorne, as he studied it, that the vessel was growing from smallness to larger size. At length, when it was as big, or bigger, than an average spaceship, its increase ceased. Quorne waited, fascinated, as an airlock opened and space-suited figures appeared.

Apparently they walked on two legs and had two arms, but the suits prevented him discovering anything further. They glanced about them, studied the asteroid for a moment, and then began to move toward the 'spaceship laboratory'. Quorne drew his proton gun in readiness. Gaining the outer airlock of the 'spaceship laboratory' they hammered upon it. Quorne did not move.

Then the men, if men they were, walked straight through the solid tungsten-steel door and appeared on the other aide, stepping incredibly out of the metal and thereby disproving one of the basic laws of physics— that no two states of matter can occupy the same place at the same time without, of course, producing an inconceivably violent explosion and irresistible expansion of energy.

There were four men, Quorne noted, as he recovered from the shock. He kept his gun steady but did not fire it. Through their helmets the men eyed him fixedly and he was able to detect the most fearsome faces he had ever encountered. They were inhumanly square, with enormous, tightly shut mouths. Noses were absent, but there were two fleshy slits that could have passed for air passages. Instead of two eyes they had one, and this in the centre of the enormous forehead. It was round, lidless, and stared with baleful intensity.

The four men snapped back their helmets on hinges

and revealed their faces. They were still revolting, and total baldness did not help. The general picture was one of pitiless scientific intelligence completely divorced from human characteristics.

Then one of them spoke, using English with the precision of just having learned it. His voice was fairly musical and like ordinary human beings. It appeared that he had no teeth, even though he articulated correctly.

"From the equipment around you, and the tale your mind has to tell, you are the man we seek," the creature announced.

"Indeed?" Quorne slowly gathered confidence again. "I am Sefner Quorne of Jupiter, and naturally I am only too pleased to make the acquaintance of brother scientists. I am not certain of what part of the Universe you come from," Quorne continued. "Nature is so bountiful with her worlds: one cannot have knowledge of all of them."

"We do not come from any world in this Universe, Sefner Quorne."

"No? Then from a greater universe, I take it? The macrocosm?"

CHAPTER SEVENTEEN
PUZZLED TRIO

There was no immediate answer and, as he pondered, Quorne recalled how he had seen the space machine— if such it was—appear to become larger until it had reached maximum.

"I have misunderstood," he added. "Clearly you have come from a smaller universe."

"Not entirely," said the spokesman. "We came *via* an atomic universe, certainly, but we are from another dimensional universe, from the world of Ur. I am Mozan, the selected leader of this expedition, but not the ruler of our world. He died—so did nearly all our race—because of you."

"Because of me?" Quorne repeated blankly. "But what had I to do with it? I never knew there was such a world as Ur!"

"That we grant you—but you destroyed nearly all its population."

"But how could that be?"

Mozan said: "Some survivors set off from their denuded world to find the perpetrator of disaster, it clearly having come from a gigantic universe outside our own. The only way to reach it was in a machine capable of infinite expansion, which would finally break the bounds of its known universe and expand into the one beyond. You are aware, of course, that all creation is composed of Universes within Universes, from the mightiest to the smallest, and all controlled in their ordered courses by the Supreme Mathematician upon whom none has ever looked?"

"Certainly I am aware of it," Quorne retorted, irritated, putting his gun away.

Mozan of Ur said: "I repeat, we set off to find the perpetrator of disaster. Twelve machines began the journey: only one finished the course, carrying us. That we have found you is sufficient reward for our trip."

"I have not perpetrated anything," Quorne said. "Or if I did, it was in total ignorance."

"Ignorance is no excuse and we do not accept it. Molith of Ur, who has succeeded to the title of ruler on our planet, wishes to pass judgement upon you, and for that reason you shall come back with us to our world."

Quorne's heliotrope eyes gleamed. "I think you underrate me, Mozan. I shall not go anywhere unless it is of my own free will."

"The time ratio between this universe and our own differs, of course," Mozan remarked, "otherwise we could not have crossed an entire universe so quickly. But when we arrive back, the return journey will reverse the time differences, and in our world of Ur very little time will have elapsed. I would add that it was during our journey here that we learned your language, chiefly from recordings made of broadcast speeches."

Quorne said: "What am I supposed to have done to your world?"

"You did it by destructive thought waves—unknowingly, but that will not permit you to escape the penalty."

"Thought waves? But I—"

"From your mind," Mozan interrupted, "it becomes apparent that, several of your Earth weeks ago, you launched a vast wave of destructive thoughts toward the planet Earth. You did not stop to consider, of course, that those same thoughts could reach other universes in their track! Our world received the thought waves with such devastating effect that, as I have said, three-quarters of our race died. We are ready to leave. Come."

Quorne whipped out his gun and gave a desperate glance through the port toward the asteroid.

"I am not going," he retorted. "And you cannot make me!"

The single eyes of the men of Ur fixed on Quorne with relentless intensity. Powerful though his own mind was, it was not capable of holding four alien brains at bay, with the result that his gun finally dropped from his nerveless fingers and a blank look came over his face.

"Get into a spacesuit," Mozan ordered, and waited while Quorne mechanically obeyed. This done, the men of Ur dropped their helmets back into position, opened the airlock door, and pushed Quorne out ahead of them. In a few minutes they gained their own vesel, but so completely was Quorne's mind subjected he took not the least interest in his surroundings.

Sealing the airlock opening, Mozan then moved to the switchboard and operated a control. Immediately, around the ship, there glowed a pale yellow shell of energy, expanding with the moments until it had encompassed an area half a mile in diameter, which included the synthetic asteroid in which the *Ultra* was still sealed.

Within the *Ultra* the Amazon, Abna, and Viona had about arrived at the point where their inactivity was becoming irksome.

"It's time we did something!" the Amazon declared. "Plainly Quorne has given up his attempt, evidently assuming we've been crushed. By this time he may be halfway back to Earth, ready to start something new. Are you ready to try to mentally move this rock prison hemming us in, Abna?"

"Certainly I am." He crossed to the Amazon's side. Viona also took up position—all three of them being in front of the thought-amplifying projectors, and then the Amazon hesitated.

Almost immediately Abna and Viona realized why. The *Ultra* was quivering spasmodically.

"He's started again!"

Abna crossed to the nearest obliterated porthole. There was only the rock solidity apparently, but something strange was happening to it. Instead of it remaining flat against the tough glass, moving imperceptibly inwards under the ever-accumulating pressure, it was drawing away.

"What do you make of it?" the Amazon asked, studying the matter for herself. "It looks as though this rock is expanding outwards, causing us to become loosened in the centre—or else we are becoming smaller, which is ridiculous."

"I don't understand this at all," Abna declared. "Do you notice a queer tingling feeling? Like static electricity?"

"I've noticed it for some time," the Amazon replied. "Can't be anything within our vessel here, because all the power is switched off."

Realizing with the advancing seconds that they were in the midst of the greatest mystery yet, the trio remained at the window. By degrees, the rock that had hemmed them in became so far distant as to disappear, but the most extraordinary thing was that the Plutonian landscape did not make itself apparent in its place.

"Just where are we?" Viona asked, perplexity in her blue eyes. "From the look of things we are in space—and yet we can't be!"

"Don't be too sure of that," Abna replied, peering intently into the utter blackness. "Unless I'm very much mistaken, there are stars appearing—slowly."

He was right. As the seconds crept onward and that sensation of static tingling continued, stars began to clearly make themselves evident, until at last everywhere was powdered in them. And not only stars. There were nebulae, distant galaxies, island universes—the whole inconceivable agglomeration of the infinite.

"Space!" More puzzled than she had ever been in her life, the Amazon gazed upon the vastness. "And we're floating free in the midst of it."

From the stars outside, it was forced upon them that they were not in any space they could recognize. There were no familiar stars or constellations.

"This is incredible!" the Amazon declared. "Even the detector, always set on Earth in case we lose our way, is not registering—which means we must be an inconceivable distance away from it! Why, even when I was once hurled into the deeps of space, the detector still operated faintly. I don't understand—"

"I believe I do," Abna interrupted, gazing into the void. "Cut off the lights for a moment, Vi."

She did so and the scene without became correspondingly brighter. Abna pointed.

"Look—over there. A pencil-shaped speck on the move. See it?"

"Spaceship, apparently," the Amazon said.

She swung the telescopic equipment into action and peered through the lens. Her wonderment deepened as she studied the vessel.

"I've never seen one like it before," she said when at length she gave the instrument over to Abna. "It certainly isn't one from our own Solar System."

Abna swung the x-ray equipment into focus with the telescope and again surveyed the far distant vessel, and this time its walls were easily penetrated and revealed what lay beyond. Abna whistled softly with amazement—and when they, too, had looked, the Amazon and Viona gazed at him blankly.

"Quorne! And a captive!" the Amazon exclaimed,

"And those creatures with him are utterly unlike anybody we've yet encountered," Viona added. "What's the answer, do you think?"

"Only one that I can think of," Abna replied. "We become so small, I believe, that tens of millions of people the size of us could have easily find room on the point of a needle."

"What!" the Amazon exclaimed. "You mean we're in the microcosm?"

"Not now—but we came *via* the infinite small, and have emerged into another universe in a higher dimension. That's the way it looks, taking all the facts into account. First the asteroid fell away from us as, presumably, we became smaller, caused no doubt by the asteroid—being artificial matter—shrinking at a far less pace than us and the *Ultra*. After that, as we became smaller and smaller still, we fell through a wormhole, and then emerged into this other space."

The Amazon frowned. "But we can't be in a microcosmic universe, surely? Atomic nuclei are *not* miniature solar systems! Such a resemblance is only because of the similarity of relative distances between particles—electrons orbiting a proton being toughly similar to that of a planet around a sun. But there the resemblance ends!"

Abna smiled. "There is much yet that we do not understand about the atomic realm, Vi. At the micro level the laws of physics can change. For instance, we have long suspected that gravity is a relatively weak force, because it has been leaking into other universes outside our own, into higher dimensions, perhaps through miniature wormholes. Gravity is vastly stronger at the micro level, buckling space to open gateways to other dimensions outside our own three. These dimensions may be 'curled up' relative to our own. It is perfectly possible that entire alien universes and solar systems exist at what *appears* to us to be the atomic level—but which are actually comparable in size to our own to their denizens in higher dimensions."

"I think," the Amazon admitted, "that you're right, Abna. But how did we get caught up as we have?"

Abna shrugged. "Presumably that vessel over there is an atom ship, not a spaceship, and its radiating waves of energy as it became smaller also affected us within the asteroid so that we became smaller, too. Obviously there are expert scientists aboard that vessel—expert enough to understand inter-atomic travel and to capture Sefner Quorne."

Then Viona asked: "How do we get back? We've no equipment for creating infinite expansion, which is the only way to return. I know that you and mother understand the principle involved, since you once burst out of our normal universe into the larger one, but in this instance...." She stopped helplessly.

"I am not so sure," the Amazon said, "that we want to go back just yet. Earth and the System can manage well enough without us for a while, and our avowed intention is to follow Quorne until we have destroyed him. The best thing we can do is watch where these scientists take him and then decide what to do."

"We must get on our way," Abna decided. "We are just drifting free in space as it is, and that vessel is getting farther and farther away. I think we might make ourselves invisible, too. Granting they haven't seen us already, it's unlikely they'll have detectors on the watch for anybody following. They probably think they're alone in space. Luckily for us, that asteroid must have hidden us from them."

The Amazon turned to the control panel and started up the power plant. Immediately the *Ultra* began moving in the general direction of the far distant atom ship. Then she activated another control so that all outflowing light-waves from the *Ultra* were stopped, rendering it invisible to outside eyes.

"I wonder why they took Quorne?" she asked, puzzled. "Or if it comes to that, I wonder why he ever allowed himself to be taken?"

"Possibly hypnosis," Abna answered. "They evidently have a very special reason for wanting him— perhaps as a specimen of life from our universe."

"Unlikely," the Amazon replied. "They are skilled scientists and I'm sure they'd never make a trip from the intra-atomic gulf just for the doubtful pleasure of taking one specimen from a dead world like Pluto. I think they must have a reason for wanting Quorne, and nobody else."

"If they dispose of him, it will save us the trouble," Viona commented.

"Not entirely." The Amazon's face was grim. "We have resolved to destroy him mentally and physically, so that he can never return. The most these scientists will do, I expect, is destroy his body and not his mental processes."

CHAPTER EIGHTEEN
UNABLE TO ESCAPE

Four days and nights of Earth time had passed before there was a sign of a change in the monotonous journeying through the deeps—and the change came when a blue-tinted world made itself apparent in the deeps. It was one of nine planets circling a sapphire blue primary. The coloring was extraordinary and, as they gazed out of the port, it turned the complexion of the trio to gray and their lips to black.

"Apparently that is home for our wandering friends," the Amazon commented. "A not unpleasant world from the look of it, except for the ghastly color scheme."

The alien world swept nearer—its surface partly cloud-wreathed, but in the clear patches between there were signs of civilized cities, not unlike earthly ones, and great areas given over to the cultivation of crops.

"Down they go," Abna said, watching the atom ship sinking to one of the several cities scattered about the planet. "Head for the open country, Vi, and come down."

She brought the great machine to rest at the edge of an extensive area devoted to crops. By some process that she could hardly understand, a journey had been made from their own Universe into another one via infinite smallness. Yet everything appeared orthodox enough—a sure proof of Relativity.

Abna said: "Our object is to get Quorne and deal with him in our own way before these other people do it. The only way can do that, as far as I can see, is to temporarily range ourselves on his side until we have extricated him and can deal with him in our own way."

"Never!" the Amazon snapped. "I'll die before I'll pose as a friend of his."

"I didn't say treat him as a friend."

Viona hurried to the storage locker and began to set out a meal. Abna reflected for a while as the Amazon inspected her gun in readiness for later action.

"I'm particularly interested in finding out why Quorne was taken," Abna remarked. "And it will also be necessary for us to find the equipment to enlarge ourselves back to our own Universe. We can do it in no other way than going to the city."

Immediately the meal was over, the trio set off in the direction of the distant city. Of itself the journey was not unpleasant, even though the blue sun was extremely bewildering, after being accustomed to a golden one. The sky appeared purple-black in consequence, but the density of the air—quite breathable—prevented any stars making themselves apparent.

Then, unexpectedly, as the three were making up their minds what they would do when they reached the city, their surroundings dissolved from around them.

The obscurity did not prevail for long, and when it lifted they were in some kind of huge stone chamber with massive colonnades.

At the far end of the room, lying amidst cushions, a figure stirred and motioned.

"Come forward, please," he invited.

The three obeyed warily, the Amazon keeping her hand on her gun. At length they reached the reclining figure. He wore long vestments of what seemed to be satin with a considerable quantity of queer jewellery hanging from his neck. He was revolting to look at with the single relentless eye, the absence of nose, and a steel trap of a mouth.

"Be seated," he commanded, and the trio relaxed into soft cushions and waited, their eyes straying to guards whom they had just noticed in the shadows by the far wall. The single blue light overhead, sunken into the lofty roof, was so designed that its effulgence descended on this mysterious and apparently extremely lazy being.

"I trust you will forgive my using the fourth dimension to bring you here," the recumbent creature apologized. "But, as you will understand, we cannot permit unknowns to wander at will about our world. It is something of a problem how you come to be here at all, but to judge from our instruments you used invisibility to make your approach and then cast it aside because you had to. That was when you become appreciable to us."

"Who are you, and where are we?" the Amazon asked flatly.

"I am Molith, and this is the world of Ur. I gather from your thoughts that you must be the three of whom Sefner Quorne spoke—the three whom he hates so bitterly."

"Yes, we are the enemies of Quorne," the Amazon said. "He is a destroyer of worlds and—"

"Exactly—a destroyer of worlds, which is why we took so hazardous a journey—or at least my comrades did—to seek him out. He is to pay the extreme penalty for wiping out three-quarters of our race with his thought waves."

"Could you explain more fully?" the Amazon asked, puzzled.

Molith told the story as Mozan had told it to Quorne.

"Very remarkable," Abna commented. "So his destructive thought waves penetrated this far, leaking into your dimension via a rift in the infinite small."

"Correct. Unfortunately for us—and for him—our universe lay in the track of those thought waves, and the results were devastating. However, you need have no fear that we hold any hostility toward you. Quite the contrary, since it appears you have been as wronged by Sefner Quorne as we have. Under those circumstances perhaps we may consider that we have bridged time and space and can exchange notes?"

The Amazon nodded. "Very well. I am prepared to tell you anything you wish to know about our System and Universe, if in return, you will guarantee me a complete electronic formula of how we may return to our own space."

"You mean you have no knowledge of the laws of infinite expansion and contraction?"

"When in my own Universe, yes. Here, no. The basic equations will be different, and without a knowledge of them we cannot find our way back."

"From your mind," the ruler of Ur said, "I realize that is the truth. But forgive me if I should place words wrongly here and there. I only learned your language at all through reading Sefner Quorne's mind."

"I am surprised that he left his mind open enough for you to do that," Abna remarked.

"He had no choice. Ever since capture his mind has been in subjection, chiefly because he is too dangerous for it to be allowed freedom."

"You haven't answered my question, Molith," the Amazon reminded him.

Molith smiled, and it was particularly hideous. "Do you not think, Golden Amazon, that I would be a fool indeed to give you three the knowledge of how to come and go in our Universe? Already one from your Universe has all but destroyed us. Do you imagine I would take such a risk again? If you do not know the way back, that is your misfortune. You will not be harmed by us: you can move as you will. Certainly you will not learn anything, because we are too scientifically shielded for that. I think the best thing you can do is to make up your minds to stay in this Universe for the rest of your lives. You have your free choice of planets and your own spaceship in which to travel to them. I cannot be fairer than that."

The Amazon tightened her lips and gave Abna a glance. He was staring fixedly at Molith, trying to read from his labyrinth of a brain something of the formula that was needed—but he failed. Molith sensed what was happening and blanked his thoughts completely.

"I suppose," the Amazon asked, for want of something better to say, "that you have decided upon a fate for Sefner Quorne?"

"Certainly. He is to die!"

"In what way? I would warn you that destroying Quorne's body would not be the slightest use. His mind is greater than his body and will reform a body around it if necessary. If you do not destroy that mind, you can never be sure but what Quorne will return.... For that matter, the same might be said of any of us here."

"I am aware of your mental power, my friends, and of that of Sefner Quorne. However, the decease that we have planned for him will be absolute. His mind and his body will be infinitely expanded until every atom is forced asunder by a gulf of countless billions of electronic miles, making it impossible for cohesion and attraction to ever form again. His mind, which is but a process of highly sensitive electrons of a different order to that of matter, will undergo the same process and no reunity will ever be possible. Fragmentary sections of his mind and body will be scattered about this Universe, some of them perhaps even breaking through to the universe beyond—yours."

"That certainly sounds efficient," the Amazon agreed, a curiously subdued excitement in her voice. "I don't think we could have devised anything better, or even as good."

"I am flattered," Molith replied drily.

Silence. Molith's single hypnotic eye roved over the three faces, striving to penetrate into their minds, and failing. Finally he shrugged.

"Well, my friends, if you have information concerning your Universe which you would like to give to me, I—"

"Certainly not," the Amazon interrupted. "You choose to withhold from us the formula we need, so we shall not part with one iota of information. With your permission, we will return to our space machine and go in search of a world upon which we can settle."

"If you wish. My only regret is that we cannot be scientific friends. Surely, Golden Amazon, you can see my point of view? I am compelled to protect my own Universe, as much as you would protect yours."

The Amazon hesitated, glancing at Abna and Viona. Then she nodded slowly.

"Yes, I can see your point of view. Perhaps we can yet find a compromise. Before we come to any basis of agreement, though, I would prefer to be certain that Quorne is really eliminated in the way you have outlined. Would you permit us to be present when the annihilation takes place? We have as much reason as you to wish to see him destroyed."

"I think that could be arranged," Molith assented. "The elimination will be in three hours, as you measure time. If, in the meantime, you care to stay as my guests

I can—"

"Thank you, no," the Amazon interrupted. "We can use the time to sleep. We have not rested for a long time. With your permission, we will return here in three hours."

"Very well. Would you prefer to walk the distance back to your ship, or shall I have you four-dimensionally transported as before?"

"Transportation, I think," Abna said, as the Amazon glanced at him.

The ruler nodded and pressed a button among the maze of them inset into a section of the floor beside his cushion couch. He spoke into a concealed microphone and presumably his orders were relayed to some scientific department elsewhere in the strange Grecian-style edifice. The next thing the Amazon, Abna, and Viona knew was that they were standing only a few yards away from the *Ultra*.

CHAPTER NINETEEN
TROUBLE AHEAD

When they were inside the *Ultra*, the Amazon sealed the airlock and switched on the current that completely polarized all radiation that might try to penetrate—particularly radio pickup waves.

"I have an idea," she said, "but it will demand a great deal of caution and precision to put it into practice. We know that Quorne is to be killed by infinite expansion of his material and mental molecules. It must be some formula by which atom ships are made to expand between our dimensional universes. It can't be anything else, since the set of equations that apply to matter will equally distend an atom ship or a living body. They're both matter, though at differing rates of vibration."

Abna snapped his fingers. "You mean if we are present when Quorne is put to death, we can perhaps find a way to discover the formula which will have to be used on him?"

"Exactly! Abna, use your wits to devise a machine—within the three hours' grace we have—to automatically record the vibrations of the mathematical equations which will be used to destroy Quorne. A small machine which we can keep hidden, but which will register the figures."

Abna became lost in thought for a time; then with a nod to himself he headed into the *Ultra*'s laboratory and looked about him upon the immense supply of materials. The Amazon and Viona followed him in, watching expectantly.

"I can do it," he said briefly, "provided both of you help me to the limit, doing exactly as you're told and not asking any questions. I just haven't time to give replies. Quickly—two drums of copper wire and two small-sized rheostats...."

So he began his tremendous race against time, using every ounce of his scientific skill in the creation of a remarkable device, which, as it began to take shape, looked rather like a cross between a watch and a compass. It was the internal workings that were so sensitive, electrical points being so small as to need a microscope to determine how to fit them into place. Here and there, where even the microscope could not handle the matter, Abna used mind force to slide nearly infinitesimal terminals into position.

Neither the Amazon nor Viona could judge what he was about. They just did as they were told, but at the close of two and a half hours Abna announced that the job was complete and held it up. The object was circular, of solid gold, and no bigger or thicker than a watch.

"Certainly it looks like a masterpiece," the Amazon

said, "but how does it work? Are you even sure that it will?"

"Certain. For instance...." He moved across to the nearest computer and switched it on. Then into the almost-human brain of the instrument he fed the question: "What is the speed of light in a vacuum?"

The apparatus hummed and instantly a display showed the figures: 299,792.5 km per sec.

Abna took the detector from his pocket and, pressing the concealed button upon it, caused the plain gold front to snap back. On the complicated set of figure window had appeared the numbers 299,792.5, and in a lower window the "second" slot had produced the figure 1.

"Simple enough," he said, as he turned the numbers back to zero. "Numbers give forth a vibration, starting at the digit one and increasing thereafter as the power of the total increases. All this little instrument does is pick up those nearly undetectable vibrations, step them up through a minute transformer, and then registers them—stopwatch fashion. The multiple windows are so that we can deal with multi-billions if need be—and this section here is for equations whereby a mass of figures is simplified to a common denominator. Which, I think, is exactly what we want."

"A masterpiece!" the Amazon exclaimed in delight. "I knew you could do it, Abna. And it operates even if in the pocket!"

"Certainly. Molith won't have the slightest suspicion. And now we ought to be on our way. I'm trusting that

Molith will see us emerge from this ship and give us one of his handy four-dimensional lifts to his abode."

Such proved to be the case and the familiar mists enveloped them when they were only a few yards from the *Ultra*. When they emerged again in the Grecian hall of Molith, they found him waiting, and this time attired in different and more close-fitting garments.

"Greetings," he acknowledged briefly. "This way."

The guards from the shadows closed in a wide circle and followed their master and the trio from the room, down a corridor, and then into a metal-walled laboratory of immense size. In the centre of it, clear of all instrument panels, was a tall stand with a gleaming pillar in the centre of it. To the pillar's summit were attached thick cables that led back to electromagnets. And at the pillar's base stood Sefner Quorne, firmly shackled with chain. He gave a start as he saw the trio, then the cold smile came to his hatchet-features.

"This must be quite a triumphal sight for you," he commented.

"It is," the Amazon agreed. "My only regret is that I was not responsible for your capture.... And you are to be congratulated on revealing no surprise at seeing us here."

"No reason why I should. Molith told me of your arrival, and of your intention to witness my decease. I have fought a hard battle, and lost it. To you three go the honors, though what use they will be to you, lost in this universe, I do not know."

None of the trio made any response, and Molith

made a signal to the men grouped before the switchboards and they started the generators. The Amazon, Abna, and Viona waited, all of them thinking at that moment of the detector in Abna's pocket. It seemed that he was close enough to the switchboards for their mathematical vibrations to reach him.

"For what is now going to happen to you, Sefner Quorne, I have no regrets," Molith said. "You have been proven a destroyer, and must, in turn, be destroyed.... Proceed," he finished, and immediately the men at the switchboards went into action.

No sound escaped Quorne, defiant to the last, as livid electrical bolts flashed and exploded around him. He became veiled in an aura of lavender lights, and as they expanded their area he expanded also, larger and larger, until he was bigger than the pillar, as big as the laboratory. At last he was nothing more than a vastly attenuated mist which evaporated slowly and left behind a sensation of tremendous strain and electrical reaction. Molith did not give the order for the technicians until half an hour later. When the hum of the generators ceased everything seemed incredibly, painfully quiet.

"That is the finish," Molith said. "Our instruments show that the mind and body of Sefner Quorne have distended to the greatest possible maximum and can never again form into union, except in the rare case of the process being reversed, of course, which will not happen."

"Definitely not," the Amazon agreed. "There is

nothing left for us to do, then, but thank you for permitting us to see the extinction of our enemy. Now we shall be on our way—to a different world, to decide our future when we get there."

Molith bowed gravely and made yet another signal to his colleagues. Accordingly the four-dimensional system came into operation and the trio found themselves within a few yards of the *Ultra*. They kept silent, controlling their emotions as much as possible and overcoming the temptation to run pell-mell to the *Ultra*. They finally gained its airlock after a leisurely walk and passed inside. Then, the moment the airlock was shut, Abna quickly yanked the detector from his pocket and snapped open the front.

After a few moments' study of the maze of figures, every window being filled with them, he snapped his fingers in delight.

"Got it! Positively got it!" he exclaimed. "In an hour I should be able to work out the formula, with the help of the computer banks."

"Then we'd better get on the move and do it some distance from this planet," the Amazon decided.

Abna was too eagerly concentrating on the figures in the detector to notice particularly what she was saying—so she crossed to the control board, started the power plant, and in a few moments had the machine heading out into the void, away from the blue primary. When at length she had settled upon a course, she put the automatic pilot in position and went to join Abna and Viona in the laboratory.

Both of them were busy with sheets of figures, which Viona constantly fed to the computers. They in turn worked out sections of the formula from the basic figures given. So finally, when the hour was up, Abna gathered together the sum total of the computers' findings and worked out the final details.

"Done it!" he announced finally. "Every figure checks—but it will mean a complete conversion of our power plant, Vi. It will have to be dismantled and then reset. It's a matter of conversion from atomic power to electronic vibration, and instead of the power all being used for propulsion, it will have to extend in an aura about us instead. That means carrying power cables to every part of the machine so that all of it will be affected. The basis of the whole is that the electronic orbits making up the vessel, and ourselves, of course, have to be made to expand indefinitely."

Abna got to his feet actively. "We begin by stripping the power plant and cruising free in space while we do it. Our course is clear of foreign attractions, Vi, isn't it?"

"Entirely clear," she assented, leading the way to the control room.

So the task began whilst the *Ultra* cruised steadily through the wastes of space to nowhere in particular. All three were aware of the considerable risk they were running for, if some strongly gravitational body happened to present itself and claim the ship by its mass, there would be nothing they could do about it with the power-plant stripped. It was just one of the chances they had to take, and at intervals the Amazon anxiously studied the view outside, and on each occasion did not see anything within measurable distance which could cause trouble. As for Ur, it had long since vanished into remoteness, and so had the blue sun.

Once the power plant was in pieces, the conversion to electronic vibration components was not a particularly long task in the laboratory. By far the longer job was that of wiring every part of the vessel so that the current could be uniformly carried. The Amazon and Viona undertook this task while Abna did the power plant conversion. They were in the midst of it when one of the Amazon's studies of the outer scene through the port revealed possible danger infinitely far ahead. There loomed a planetary system and a primary. Evidently stellar systems were more closely ranged together in this sector of the alien cosmos.

"I don't like the look of that," the Amazon said, worriedly, as Viona joined her in gazing outside. "Tell your father to rush the conversion through with all speed."

Viona did so, but the task was such that rushing it was not possible, with the result that the minutes crept by and wiring of the vessel continued—and the planetary system came ever closer. At its present speed, without any means of turning aside, nothing could prevent the *Ultra* hurtling straight into the system and grinding itself to powder.

"How long do you estimate before we reach that system?" Abna called from the laboratory.

"At our present speed about forty-five minutes," the Amazon answered.

"Then we've got to think of something quickly. I shan't be ready with this for at least two hours, and then it has to be put together again."

"Only one answer," the Amazon said. "I've done it before so I can try it again. Carry on with the wiring, Viona, and leave this other problem to me."

The girl nodded, though she looked vaguely wondering. Turning to the locker the Amazon quickly donned a spacesuit, then from the armoury rack she took down the most powerful protonic cannon in the array. Strapping it over one shoulder, she made her way to the emergency ladder and so through the roof airlock to the summit of the *Ultra*.

CHAPTER TWENTY
BACK IN 'FORM'

For a moment or two she was busy with the lifeline, securing it to the base of the *Ultra*'s conning tower and surveying the infinite wastes of space around her as she did so. The effect was precisely the same as if she were in normal space in her own Universe. The laws of mass and gravity were not one whit different.

When the lifeline was secure, she made her way to the nose of the vessel and began to walk down it, always perpendicular to its surface since it was her only attraction—though seen from the roof she would have appeared to be horizontal, her helmeted head projecting into space.

When she reached this position, she put the protonic cannon to her shoulder and pressed the button. A stream of deadly fire slashed into infinity in front of her—but this did not signify. It was the tremendous recoil kick the cannon had which mattered. Her body was strong enough to take it as she was jolted backwards. Deliberately she kept her legs braced for the strain, with the result that the entire *Ultra* beneath her moved too, swinging in free space. There was nothing miraculous about the feat; it simply meant that the *Ultra* had no other opposing gravitation to prevent its movement, and no resistance whatever to its tremendous forward velocity.

Satisfied, the Amazon tried again—and again, and every time she fired the cannon the huge vessel swung its nose farther around, until at last it was at right angles to the system looming in the distance. That was all that was needed. Still retaining its initial velocity—or almost, since the act of turning had expended energy which had slowed it very slightly—it was now moving away from the menacing system into what appeared to be the endless wastes of space where no danger threatened. And even if it did, the Amazon was prepared to 'punt' the giant *Ultra* onto a new course again until safety was assured.

Breathing hard, she returned into the vessel, dumped the cannon, and pulled off her space suit. Viona, practically at the end of the wiring task, gave her an admiring glance.

"That was a marvellous feat, mother. I'd never have thought of it."

"In a tight corner you would," the Amazon smiled. "Just the age-old law of recoil and mass made practical."

"The wiring is practically finished," Viona said. "The rest is up to father now."

The Amazon went in to Abna and found him in the midst of wiring the final armatures. Even when this was done, they had to be tested. His original estimate of two hours proved considerably wrong. It was nearer four before he had every component complete and tested to his satisfaction.

"Just a matter of reassembling now," he said, as the Amazon waited. "Grab all you can and let's get busy."

The Amazon picked up the nearest mass of weighty apparatus and walked with it into the control room, Abna coming up behind her. With Viona also to help them, the reassembling was not a difficult matter. It was linking all the multitude of wire that was the longest task, since every one had to be tabulated and screwed down into specially marked sockets.

"In some ways," Abna said, as he busied himself, "I rather regret this."

"Regret what?" the Amazon asked, surprised.

"Our leaving this alien system. I think we might have been more sensible if we'd held the formula over for a while until we really wanted to go back. In the meantime we might have enjoyed ourselves considerably exploring this alien universe. It's novel—new, worth investigating."

The Amazon shrugged. "Considering there are untold millions of worlds in our own universe which we have never even looked at, I cannot see that this space is so interesting. Besides, I'm uneasy here. It's unnatural. If we want to explore, then let it be in our own understandable Universe."

"So be it," Abna smiled. "But this space is novel just the same. To me it is quite a great thought that the entrance to this universe is to be found via the infinitely small, I think we might have found far more interesting revelations, far more concerning the underlying nature of the Universes within Universes if we'd stayed and explored."

"We didn't—and we're going home," the Amazon replied flatly. "Sorry, Abna, but this region unnerves me."

That being the case, Abna said no more and the reassembling of the power plant continued steadily. A break was made for a meal and a rest, and then the task was resumed, until at last it was completed.

"Ready," he said. "Here we go back home."

Moving to the switchboard, he tugged down the huge blades of the master switch and jammed them home. It was surprising that there was no brief flash of blue sparks. The blades engaged in their slots without a hint of electrical contact. Silent, the Amazon and Viona looked about them but there was no evidence of anything happening.

"What's wrong?" the Amazon demanded, puzzled—then she went to the converted power plant and studied it. Everything was as it should be, even to the new block of copper that was to provide the necessary energy.

Baffled, Abna looked about him, then he went into a thorough examination of all connecting points, checking them with his sheets of figures. Finally he sighed.

"As far as the wiring is concerned there are no mistakes. No doubt of that. Possibly we are not using enough power, so double it, Vi."

Promptly the Amazon brought another block of copper and fixed it in the matrix. The moment she did so, however, she gave a hoarse gasp of pain and almost instantly she shrank with bewildering rapidity—smaller, smaller, gone!

Abna stared at the spot where she had been. "The current! It must have been on!"

He and Viona swung and stared at the blades still in contact. Apparently the current had been in being, though not showing any evidence of it on the instruments because they were not geared to this particular type of energy and there had been no time to reassemble them.

"Quick!" Viona shouted frantically. "Cut off the power! Mother may still be decreasing into—into I don't know what!"

Abna leaped, seized the switch handle, and disengaged the blades.

"What do we do now?" Viona asked helplessly. "What went wrong, father? I don't understand it."

"I do—now," he replied grimly. "This current, the way we have wired it, is in an inverse ratio, one of the trickiest mathematical formulae to work out. And it also does not operate en masse on inorganic substances. That seems clear, otherwise the ship would have responded, except that it would have shrunk instead of expanding. To work out the puzzle of inverse ratio—to make expansion take the place of contraction—is a job that will take the computers several days. Your mother, being organic, was instantly affected and shrank beyond the vanishing point.

"Infernal bungling!" he breathed in fury. "This is what comes of trying to work out a formula from a few scattered truths! I'd have seen the mistake had I had more time in which to do it."

"But what about mother?" Viona insisted. "We've got to rescue her...."

"You mean I have," Abna interrupted. Moving forward, he locked at the power plant and the copper block that the Amazon had dropped when she had shrunk: then he turned to Viona and put an arm about her shoulder. "Viona, you, have an unpleasant task to perform," he said gently. "You must stay here while I go and look for your mother."

"Stay here alone? Never! I'm coming with you!"

"You can't. Somebody has to stay and look after the machine. While I am gone, give the computers the basic figures of this formula and tell them to reverse it. That will show you exactly how to reset the wiring so that enlargement takes place instead of contraction. We'll have to find how to make inorganic substance responsive, but that can come later. When the wires are reset, switch on the power. Its influence should reach your mother and me and we should return. If we do not...."

Abna became silent, smiling gently as he saw tears in the girl's eyes.

"Cheer up, youngster," he murmured. "We'll come back, never fear. Now, put on the current. I am going to repeat your mother's actions, which, I trust, will take me approximately to wherever she may be. It's going to hurt, I expect, but I'm ready for it."

Mechanically, Viona switched on the power and then stood aside, white-faced and tight-lipped, as her father deliberately grasped the two opposite poles of the power matrix. The savagery of the pain that lashed him nearly overcame his senses for a moment—then it was gone as his body diminished to such smallness that he could no longer hold the matrix. A sensation of endless sinking was within him and the world seemed to be flying outwards as he went down and still down into remote smallness as the current within him ran its course.

He saw Viona loom gigantic. Her shoes became so enormous that they towered seeming miles over his head. The lights in the roof receded into distant stars. Then the shrinkage ceased and he moved slowly.

"Vi!" he called. "Vi, are you there?"

He peered into what seemed to be starlit darkness. He was in a deep depression on a vast, ridged plain. It came to him presently that this depression was a tiny air hole in the metal flooring of the *Ultra*'s control room, and that the plain itself was the floor, receding away to the indistinguishable walls. He was tiny, yes, inconceivably so, even in this world of the infinite small, but apparently he had not shrunk so much as to fall through the interstices of matter itself.

A sound caught his attention and he swung around quickly.

"Abna!" The dim figure of the Amazon came stumbling through the gloom. She clung to him tightly when at last she reached him. "Abna! Thank heaven! I was beginning to fear I'd really ditched myself this time."

"Are you hurt?"

"Not particularly. I was to start with when I got the shock from the matrix. I've never been so surprised in my life. What happened?"

Abna explained the matter as he had to Viona and the Amazon gave a sigh.

"So that's it! We worked on inverse ratio. And we stay here until Viona has the right answer and changes the wiring?"

"That's about the size of it. Just as well we had a meal not very long ago. It looks like we will be a while down here."

"I've been trying to imagine where we are. Any idea?"

"Certainly. This is the control room floor. We're in a hole in the metal, the size of a pinhead and about as deep, maybe. Our only light comes from the control room's ceiling lamp—those stars way up there. Several hundreds of miles away—to us, that is—will be the laboratory where I trust Viona is now at work."

Viona was—very much so. Mastering her fears as well as she could, she fed the required formula to the mathematical computers, as her father had told her to do, then until the answer should be given there was nothing for her to do but wait, and that was the difficult part. Courage she normally had in plenty, but the conditions of the moment were unfavorably balanced against her. She was in an unknown universe in a machine that could not be controlled if it ran into trouble; and her parents could never return unless she did her job with absolute exactitude.

Disconsolate, troubled, she wandered about the laboratory for a while and then went back into the control room and sat staring at the floor beside the power plant where her mother and father had disappeared. For her to distinguish them in the air-bubble was quite impossible, just as it was impossible for the Amazon and Abna to distinguish her.

Perhaps five minutes passed as she sat and pondered moodily, listening half detachedly to the very faint hum of the computers in the nearby laboratory—then she looked up sharply as something, she, knew not what, began to take shape in the air in front of her. At first it was only a mist, forming not far from the power plant. She sprang to her feet eagerly, convinced that it was either her father or mother returning.

Seconds passed and the shape became a man in a space explorer's suit. The blurred outlines ran into each other and took on sharpness. Black hair first, then a hatchet-face, and at last steady heliotrope eyes. Viona stumbled backwards as though she had received a blow.

"It—it can't be!" she shouted hysterically. "You can't be Sefner Quorne! You're dead! Disintegrated!"

"I was," Quorne replied, glancing about him in some bewilderment; then he crossed to the switchboard and pulled out the engaged blades, which, in her crisis,

Viona had neglected to do.

"Keep away from me!" she ordered, whipping out her gun.

"Very well." Quorne gave a shrug. "Believe me, though, this is as big a surprise to me as to you. I was totally extinct, in the abysmal darkness which comes when thought itself is destroyed. Then, incredibly enough, I began to reintegrate. I shrank. I returned— here. Why? At least tell me that."

CHAPTER TWENTY-ONE
AN EVEN START

Viona only glared at him and his eyes pensively studied hers. Then he gave his thin smile.

"Thanks, Viona. I have read from your mind what happened. So your mother and father have accidentally flung themselves into minutia, have they? You left the current on but it would not affect them once they had released their hold on the power plant. But it affected me and reversed the process that originally enlarged me to the point of annihilation. That is only logical since the formula was identical, but in reverse. So I returned to here, the source of the energy.... You shouldn't have left the power on, my dear."

"No—I shouldn't," Viona admitted. "That's more than obvious now. And your theory about your return appears to be correct, Quorne. Molith of Ur did mention that nothing would ever bring you back except a reversal of the formula."

"I'm difficult to be rid of, am I not?" Quorne gave his cold smile. "And incidentally, it sounds odd for you to keep calling me Quorne. There was a time when I used to be 'Sefner' and we were very much—er—

attached to each other."

"That I refuse to believe!"

"Understandable," Quorne admitted. "But the fact remains that our union produced Sefian, who gave his life to save the Universe from destruction. But for your meddling father's mental efforts, which destroyed your memory of our association, you would be fully aware of what happened."

Viona kept her gun steady. "If you are thinking of renewing that association I would warn you to be careful. "I can shoot straight—and fast."

Quorne did not respond. He looked about him and then toward the port. He gave the slightest of starts at what he beheld. Far away in the gulf of space a solitary giant star was visible—and there was no doubt that the *Ultra* was travelling rapidly in its direction.

Quorne swung around. "How does one control this vessel?" he asked sharply.

"One doesn't. The power plant has been converted as you can see."

"You mean we've no way of guiding the thing?"

"My mother had a way, but I'm not revealing it."

"Stop acting like a silly child, Viona!" Quorne ordered. "Look out the window."

Viona hesitated, prepared for some kind of trick, then since Quorne seemed to be in earnest she did as he asked and moved to his side, gazing at the far-distant sun.

"It is more than probable," Quorne said, "that there are planets circling around that primary, but at this distance we cannot see them. The first one of them that appears directly in our path will seize the *Ultra* and pull it down to destruction. "Now—what did your mother do to guide this machine?"

"It would make no difference if I explained, because we could not do it," Viona answered. "And I can't bring mother back because there isn't time. The computers will not have finished working out this problem for some days."

Quorne sighed. "Even if there was time, I would not allow you to being your father and mother back. Since they have dropped into minutia, they can stay there. Our best course is to leave the *Ultra* in a safety machine immediately."

Viona backed away, holding her gun steadily. "You'll never get me to go anywhere with you, Quorne, and I'm certainly not going to leave this vessel. Mother and father are aboard it somewhere, even though we can't see them."

Lunging forward abruptly, Quorne caught at the girl's wrists, deflecting the stream of fire that jetted from her gun. The next moment he realized that Viona had lost none of that stupendous strength which was the heritage of her parents. With her free hand she gripped the belt about Quorne's waist and whirled him from his feet, toppling him over her shoulder. He struggled up again and received two smashing blows in the face that flattened him. The next thing he knew was that he had been picked up bodily, struggling vainly high over the girl's head as she carried him down the main corridor and finally flung him into the storage hold. Slamming the door upon him, she pushed across the bolts and then hurried into the laboratory.

There was no sign yet of the computers having finished their computations. As Abna had said, it would probably take them several days—and there just was not the time. In a few hours at the most the *Ultra* would crash into that system far ahead and that would finish everything. So Viona made her plans and carried them out. She switched off the computers, which could now never produce the result in time, and then went into the safety-ship hangar where lay the two one-man space machines, only large enough to carry one person lying down.

Deliberately she went to work on first one and then the other to completely ruin the power plants so they could never be used without extensive repair. This done, she returned to the control room.

From the locker she took three spacesuits and laid them on the floor. To the belts she attached all the provisions and weapons she could locate, and there, for the moment, left them.

Surveying the scene outside, she gave a start of alarm. The distant nuclear sun had grown considerably together with several planets circling it, The nearest world, straight in the path of the *Ultra*, was of considerable size and would inevitably draw the vessel as it came near. In an hour, or even less, the *Ultra* would crash.

Quickly Viona turned back to the spacesuits and

scrambled into one of them, strapping the remaining two to her shoulders. Then she crossed to the instrument panel and closed the power switch. Reaching the copper matrix, she hesitated for a moment, then gripped the opposing electrodes. Pain brought her to her knees and she went tumbling down into whirling dark to finish up flat on her back with a solitary star infinitely high above.

Gradually pain left her and she scrambled to her feet—just as two figures came hurrying toward her in the gloom.

"Mother! Father!" she exclaimed thankfully, when she had opened her helmet.

"And what is the meaning of this?" Abna demanded angrily. "I told you to remain above! How do you suppose we are ever going to get back to—"

"We never are. The ship's going to crash first. Besides, there's Quorne, too—"

"Quorne!" the Amazon cried. "What are you talking about?"

Quickly Viona gave every detail and her father and mother kept glancing at each other anxiously in the dim light.

"So that's the situation," she finished worriedly. "In less than an hour the *Ultra* will be smashed to pieces—and Quorne with it, I hope. He can't escape because I've wrecked the safety machines. Not that I think he'll manage to get out of the storage hold anyway. I did the only thing I could. Came into smallness to find you and brought you space suits. If we survive the *Ultra's* crash we may find ourselves on a planet where there's no air. I couldn't do anything else."

"She's right," the Amazon said at last. "There was no other move she could make— But Quorne! That he should come back when the formula was reversed—!"

"Quickly—into these spacesuits," Viona urged. "We may hit that planet at any moment. I don't expect we'll survive it, but you might be able to help, father, with mind tactics."

"Our smallness might save us," he replied, struggling into the rubber-and-metal mesh. "But I don't think it will save Quorne. Not that the crash will destroy his mind. It will only be his body and he'll perhaps find a way to re-create that."

"The position is grim," the Amazon commented after a moment. "We have lost the formula for enlargement: we have no spaceship, and we're lost utterly in an atomic universe with our worst enemy recreated— for the moment."

"But if he survives the crash which is coming, he will not be very far from us," Abna said. "And he knows no more how to get back to our own universe than we do. He will be normal size. We shall be infinitesimal, and therein may lie our advantage."

Neither the Amazon nor Viona had any comment to make to this, chiefly because they had not Abna's optimism.

Viona said after a while, through the audiophone when the spacesuit helmets had been closed: "Why is it that our clothes, and these spacesuits, contracted to smallness when we did? I thought you said, father, that the energy did not operate on inorganic things?"

"In the normal way it doesn't—but clothes are permeated with the energy of the person wearing them, and therefore contract with the wearer. As did those space suits which were fastened to you. With metal and similar objects no such rule applies—as we know to our cost."

"Do you hear something like thunder?" the Amazon asked abruptly, and after a while Abna and Viona grasped what she meant. There was a remote rumbling, booming noise coming from somewhere, like explosions hundreds of miles distant.

"That isn't thunder," Viona said at length. "It's Quorne, banging on the storage locker door. With us being so small the sound waves are lengthened and have a more rumbling quality—"

Whatever else she intended saying was negated by a sudden violent earthquake—or so it seemed to be. The 'plain' on which the three were standing swayed back and forth with terrific violence, flinging them from their feet. They were rolled and pitched helplessly for what seemed to be hundreds of yards, a series of vast concussions crashing into their audiophones. Then at last the disturbances ceased and they were able to look about them.

For a long time the view was inexplicable. But at least there was light—clear, yellow and warm, with a seemingly incredibly distant blue sky. Nearby stood a jagged mountain, its edges as sharp as the teeth on a saw.

"Atmosphere, apparently," Abna said, studying his belt instrument. Then he added: "Breathable! We can be rid of these spacesuits—"

Viona interrupted him, a queer note in her voice. "That isn't a mountain range to the right there, it's the remains of the *Ultra*—jagged metal edges sticking out against the sky! But how colossal it seems—and how dreadfully small we must be. This plain seems to go on forever."

Spacesuits had been removed before there were any further comments; then the Amazon spoke:

"Apparently the *Ultra* is utterly wrecked, and we, on account of our smallness, survived. Maybe we fell through a crack in the metal. We are on a world that appears inconceivably vast because we are so tiny. But we have intelligence, weapons, and some food. We can probably find our way back home—someday."

She had scarcely finished speaking before Abna gripped her arm and pulled her back. Narrowly she escaped the downward movement of something falling out of the sky, something that blocked the sunlight for a moment in the shape of a gargantuan shadow. A hill appeared magically to the left and was seen to be a heavy space boot. There was a vast leg going up to heaven and, out of sight, a torso and head.

The figure moved, a stupendous giant against the light, walking swiftly.

"Quorne," the Amazon whispered, as Goliath became remote in half a dozen strides. "He survived."

"And so did we," Abna answered. "He is huge, we are little. We are both on an unknown world. We start even."

The figure of Quorne had gone now, but his enormous black shadow was speeding away across the plain.

ABOUT THE AUTHOR

British writer JOHN RUSSELL FEARN was born near Manchester, England, in 1908. As a child he devoured the science fiction of Wells and Verne, and was a voracious reader of the Boys' Story Papers. He was also fascinated by the cinema, and first broke into print in 1931 with a series of articles in *Film Weekly*.

He then quickly sold his first novel, *The Intelligence Gigantic*, to the American magazine, *Amazing Stories*. Over the next fifteen years, writing under several pseudonyms, Fearn became one of the most prolific contributors to all of the leading US science fiction pulps, including such legendary publications as *Astounding Stories*, *Startling Stories*, *Thrilling Wonder Stories*, and *Weird Tales*.

During the late 1940s he diversified into writing novels for the UK market, and also created his famous superwoman character, The Golden Amazon, for the prestigious Canadian magazine, the Toronto *Star Weekly*. In the early 1950s in the UK, his fifty-two novels as "Vargo Statten" were bestsellers, most notably his novelization of the film, *Creature from the Black Lagoon*.

Apart from science fiction, he had equal success with westerns, romances, and detective fiction, writing an amazing total of 180 novels—most of them in a period of just ten years—before his early death in 1960. His work has been translated into nine languages, and continues to be reprinted and read worldwide.